"What do you *really* want?" she asked.

"Everything you're imagining I want. But I'm not in as big a hurry as you think."

She backed away, but the counter stopped her before she got out of his embrace. "I suppose you never have to wait long, do you? They just fall into your arms and into your bed, don't they? All those women who are thrilled to be noticed by a congressman?"

"Nothing worth having is easy to get."

"But you take it anyway."

Delaney's thumb circled slowly on the bare skin between her shoulder blades. "I like your fight. You're a strong woman, and I find that a challenge. But you're also bendable. In fact, I think you've been looking for someone to make you bend, whether consciously or not."

Her pulse fluttered. "And you think you can do it?"

"It would be my pleasure..."

Dear Reader:

We're celebrating SECOND CHANCE AT LOVE's third birthday with a new cover format! I'm sure you had no trouble recognizing our traditional butterfly logo and distinctive SECOND CHANCE AT LOVE type. But you probably also noticed that the cover artwork is considerably larger than before. We're thrilled with the new look, and we hope you are, too!

In a sense, our new cover treatment reflects what's been happening *inside* SECOND CHANCE AT LOVE books. We're constantly striving to bring you fresh and original romances with unexpected twists and delightful surprises. We introduce promising new writers on a regular basis. And we aim for variety by publishing some romances that are funny, some that are poignant, some that are "traditional," and some that take an entirely new approach. SECOND CHANCE AT LOVE is constantly evolving to meet your need for "something new" in your romance reading.

At the same time, we *haven't* changed the successful editorial concept behind each SECOND CHANCE AT LOVE romance. And we've consistently maintained a reputation for being a line of the highest quality.

So, just like the new covers, SECOND CHANCE AT LOVE romances are satisfyingly familiar—yet excitingly different—and better than ever!

Happy reading,

Ellen Edwards

Ellen Edwards, Senior Editor
SECOND CHANCE AT LOVE
The Berkley Publishing Group
200 Madison Avenue
New York, N.Y. 10016

P.S. Do you receive our SECOND CHANCE AT LOVE and TO HAVE AND TO HOLD newsletter? If not, be sure to fill out the coupon in the back of this book, and we'll send you the newsletter free of charge four times a year.

INTO THE WHIRLWIND

LAUREL BLAKE

SECOND CHANCE AT LOVE BOOK

Other Second Chance at Love books by
Laurel Blake

STORMY PASSAGE #66
STRANGER IN PARADISE #154

INTO THE WHIRLWIND

Copyright © 1984 by Laurel Blake

All rights reserved. No part of this publication may be reproduced or transmitted in any form or by any means, electronic or mechanical, including photocopy, recording, or any information storage and retrieval system, without permission in writing from the publisher.

Requests for permission to make copies of any part of the work should be mailed to: Permissions, Second Chance at Love, The Berkley Publishing Group, 200 Madison Avenue, New York, NY 10016.

First edition published July 1984

First printing

"Second Chance at Love" and the butterfly emblem are trademarks belonging to Jove Publications, Inc.

Printed in the United States of America

Second Chance at Love books are published by
The Berkley Publishing Group
200 Madison Avenue, New York, NY 10016

For Rachel and Andrew

CHAPTER ONE

THE LEAN, HOT wind swept between buildings and hit the asphalt playground belly down. Grit stung Meg Birdsong's ankles. The wind came again, and she put up a hand to hold in place the thick coil of chestnut hair at the nape of her neck. In central Illinois, early June could be whimsical. When the fifth graders of the Robert G. Ingersoll School had come out for recess twenty minutes before, spring lingered in the air. Now a bruising summer heat, so good for the distant fields of corn and soybeans, so murderous in the inner-city streets of Masefield, ruled without mercy.

"Hello, Ms. Social Worker ma'am." Jonathan joined her, blotting his forehead with a red bandanna handkerchief.

"Mr. Assistant Principal sir," Meg bantered back, knowing he wanted to hear the new title he would have in the fall.

"Still coming to dinner tonight?"

"Of course. I've already bought the dessert. It's a surprise."

"Great," Jonathan returned. "How does pasta primavera sound for my part of it?"

"Wonderful. You really must teach me to cook fancy someday." Her eyes back on the children, Meg jotted a note in her folder.

Jonathan's gaze followed hers. "Who is it, the Parker boy?"

"Yes, his aggressive behavior is increasing again. There are problems at home, and he's taking out his frustrations here. I observed him in the classroom yesterday." She tapped her chin with the eraser end of her pencil. "He's headed for trouble, all right."

"Have you talked to the parents?"

"They don't have a phone. I sent a note home, but who knows if it got there?"

Jonathan nodded. "I'm sure his behavior at school is the least of the family's worries. Well, I've got lunchroom duty coming up. See you tonight."

"Wait a minute." Meg caught his arm. "Look out there, on the street."

A knot of people approached, trailed by a gleaming black car. Tape recorders, clipboards, and cameras bristled out of the bunch.

"Somebody important?" she guessed.

Jonathan adjusted his steel-rimmed glasses and squinted. "That's right. Recognize who it is?"

The bright-eyed, snappily dressed men and women around the edges looked like PR people, Meg surmised, with a local reporter or two thrown in. The young woman in front, anxiously setting the pace, would be an aide. Aide to—

Meg studied the tall man at the center of the human whirlpool. Fame, money, power: She prided herself on not being impressed by them. Social work had taught her over and over how little they had to do with the true value of a person. Then why was she experiencing this immediate awe? Was she still vulnerable, after all her training, to his reputation, to the image he had created for himself?

"Give up?" Jonathan asked.

No, it was the man himself. He'd stand out anywhere. In a coal mine. Among heads of state. "It's Cash Delaney, isn't it?"

"Our noble congressman," Jonathan concurred, "and his lovely wife. The event itself, my dear, is called mythmaking."

The group halted outside the playground fence. Delaney, in shirtsleeves, with his tie loosened, swept an arm toward the school and declaimed into the wind. Passersby drew near. At that distance, Meg and Jonathan heard only a surflike roll of oratory.

The school bell rang, sending the fifth graders whooping and jostling into the building. A crooked line of first graders replaced them, their tiny heads bent under the weight of the sun.

"I need to get back to my desk..." But Meg couldn't take her eyes off the congressman. She had seen a hundred newspaper pictures of him and untold television footage. But seeing him in person was an experience of an entirely different order.

Cash Delaney's height was mostly in his legs, with his weight concentrated in his upper body. His heavy shoulders, barrel chest, and the thrust of his head all gave him an air of menacing physical strength. Or he would give that impression, Meg corrected herself, were it not for his smile. He possessed the quintessential public smile, which he was now demonstrating for the photographer: wide, warm, genuine (really genuine? Meg wondered), as toothsome as a Kennedy grin, and unthreateningly confident. But he didn't beg you to like him; he commanded you to do so. And made you feel lucky to have been noticed in the bargain.

"So that's charisma," she mused.

Jonathan was gently sly. "Maybe it only works on strangers. His wife isn't feeling it."

He was right. Though she held her husband's arm and kept her eyes on his face, Marcia DeWitt Delaney had clearly sent her mind to a finer, more entertaining place. To Meg, she looked like a remote and beautiful snow princess out of a Scandinavian fairy tale. Her champagne-blond hair was drawn up under a white straw hat with a single red rose at the brim; her delicate person was sheltered in a white linen suit; her feet were shod in high black-and-white spectator pumps. Perspiration wasn't one of her bodily functions. Meg, surveying her own khaki shirt, with the smudges from her struggle with the VW's fan belt that morning and the grease spot on the toe of her shoe from Jessie's dropping the fried egg at breakfast, tried to imagine a life that would allow her to wear white. She couldn't quite manage it.

"Mrs. Delaney *is* stunning," she admitted.

"And rich. And a member of the most influential dynasty in downstate politics. She has an uncle on the court of appeals. Her father held every office in the state, from dogcatcher to lieutenant governor, before he went on to Congress. Her grandfather was a senator."

"Are you saying it wasn't a love match?"

Jonathan shrugged. "The man's a political genius. Every move he makes is politically motivated."

"Which brings us to the reason he's touring our humble neighborhood." Meg frowned, recalling the newspaper stories. "Looks like they're coming in here."

The wail of a child terminated their discussion.

Atop the highest slide, a little girl in patched pink overalls crouched paralyzed. Yapping like a pack of dogs, the other children crowded around the base.

Jonathan started to move. "She's really scared."

"And I don't see Rose Switzer anywhere. I'll get her down." Meg hurried ahead.

Into the Whirlwind

She reached the slide just as another person arrived on the other side of it. For an instant flashing hazel eyes, deep-set under permanently sardonic brows, held Meg's. Then Cash Delaney transferred his attention to the hysterical child, who was now whimpering wheezily, as if she was too frightened to breathe. Stark terror pinched the little face.

"What's her name?" he asked Meg.

"I think it's—"

"Carrie honey, I'll get you down." Rose Switzer, the gym teacher, bounded up the steps of the slide. She recoiled as Carrie swung at her. "Here now, just give me your hand."

Carrie beat her heels on the slide and screamed until the cords stood out on her neck.

Rose looked down at Meg. "This is going to take a while. It happened once before." She dodged to the side as Carrie slapped at her.

"No! No! Get away!" As the child flung herself against the handrails, the slide rocked, and one of its legs was pulled out of the concrete. Children shouted in horrified glee.

The soles of Congressman Delaney's black wing tips easily found a hold on the polished slide. Kneeling just below the child, thighs pressed against the sides of the slide to hold his position, he placed the palms of his hands flat against the soles of Carrie's shoes.

"Carrie, you can slide down now."

Carrie's bellows lightened to jerky sobs. Feeling the steadying pressure, she blinked at her feet and hiccuped. Meg took in the tableau: the milling children, Delaney's group and miscellaneous onlookers bunched respectfully in the background, school personnel at the windows of the school, the photographer clicking away. Meg did a double take at Mrs. Delaney. Fairy tale princess? Right now she looked hard enough to take the nickels off a dead man's eyes to buy herself a bottle of nail polish.

Whatever she was thinking, it wasn't of a frightened child.

"Here we go," Delaney told Carrie, "non-stop." Grasping her feet, he slid slowly backward.

Carrie's face registered panic, crazier panic, resistance, astonishment, then she gave a snaggle-toothed, sheepish smile.

The congressman lifted her from the bottom of the slide and knelt down beside her. "You did it." He grinned. "You know, I suspected you could."

"Congressman, could you turn this way?" the photographer broke in.

"Let's get some more kids into this." The aide waved children around the kneeling man.

Jonathan arrived beside Meg.

"Damn!" she fumed under her breath. "This makes me mad."

"Why?"

"Well at first, I thought he simply wanted to help. He saw that although Carrie was terrified, she didn't want to be carried down like a baby. Not that anybody really needed his help, of course. But look at our hero posing. It's just a corny publicity stunt."

"Now, now."

"Really, Jonathan. I resent his using our kids for a media event. He was never interested in this school before. Or anything in the entire city, for that matter."

Jonathan tugged on an earlobe. "Don't take it personally. I told you he's a political animal, size large. He's just taking advantage of the situation. Okay?"

"Okay." Meg wrinkled her nose. What was the matter with her? "You're right. Why should I care? We'll never see him at Ingersoll again. You and I both know why he's here at all."

"Why don't you ask him about that?" Jonathan nudged her.

"You know I couldn't. I don't have the nerve."

Into the Whirlwind

Delaney was getting to his feet, nodding at something the aide was telling him.

"If only you had taken that assertiveness-training seminar..." Jonathan trailed off.

Cash Delaney was advancing upon them.

He gripped Jonathan's hand. "Cash Delaney," he announced in a gravelly baritone. "Fine school you have here."

How would you know? Meg challenged him silently. Phony. I'll bet you never heard of it until five minutes ago.

"Jonathan Weiss. I teach social studies; and this is Meg Birdsong, one of our social workers."

"Hello," Meg managed to get out.

You couldn't avoid his eyes. His hand was firm and warm. "I'm running for a fourth term in Congress. I hope I can count on your vote in November."

"That very much depends," Meg was astonished to hear herself say.

The congressman quirked an eyebrow, so that it disappeared under the thick comma of black hair falling over his forehead. "Depends on what, may I ask?"

The lines of strength and experience in his face...what would it be like to see those lines every day, to watch them change?... And his lips. Kissing them would be...her heart jumped. She had forgotten his question.

Suddenly, Mrs. Delaney was there, a hand on his sleeve. "Let's go."

"In a minute." He patted her hand without taking his eyes off Meg. "Depends on—?"

"Now," Marcia Delaney hissed, eyes skittering around for eavesdroppers. "I'm tired. Enough is enough. I told you before I agreed to—"

"Why don't you go to the car?" Something ugly had happened to Delaney's smile. "I'm going to listen to what Ms...to what Meg has to say."

Marcia Delaney gave Meg the kind of flat, inattentive

look with which one registers the existence of parking meters and fire hydrants. She stepped in front of her husband, her back to Meg, and lowered her voice further. "Either you come along, or I go straight to the *Gazette*."

Delaney's lips hardly moved. "Just because you're tired? Better save that bluff for a more important occasion."

"This has nothing to do with fatigue. I've had it, and I'm not bluffing."

"Neither am I. I came here to listen to the voters."

The rose on Marcia Delaney's hat trembled. Out of the corner of her eye, Meg saw the aide, eyes glassy with tension, intercept a reporter.

"That's it, then?" Marcia Delaney's voice got higher and softer. "No discussion?"

"We've discussed everything already, darling." Delaney loosened his tie further with weary insolence. "You run along now before you get heatstroke."

Mrs. Delaney glanced toward the street, then again at her husband and at Meg. She opened her perfectly made up lips, shut them again, and turned on her heel.

If an icicle could walk, Meg reflected, it would have Marcia Delaney's stiff, brittle gait. She looked around. Jonathan was talking to Rose Switzer. No one else was near enough to have heard the exchange.

The skin over Delaney's jaw was drawn tight. He was pale under his tan. "You were saying?"

This was no time to attack the man. "It isn't important." She started to turn away.

"Oh, but it is. More important than you know." He willed her to meet his unsettling, direct stare.

Meg swallowed hard. It was conservative politicians like Delaney who so often stood in the way of the laws and funding her families needed. At best he was her adversary; at worst, the enemy of everything she worked for. "Okay. I've been reading about your recent move into this neighborhood, into the renovated town house over on Princeton."

"Yes?" He was a king deigning to notice a whining peasant.

Was charisma merely sexual attractiveness? He was so masculine, so unbelievably sexy... no, of course there was more to it than that...

She got a grip on herself. "You've been quoted as saying that you want to live among your constituents and share their concerns. Also, you say you want to demonstrate your commitment to the renaissance of the cities and to help stop the flight to the suburbs."

"Do you see anything wrong with that?"

"No, no. Not if your motives are sincere." Out on the street, Marcia Delaney hailed a cab. What had their argument been about, anyway?

"I assure you they are." There was a thread of steel in his voice now.

"They say," Meg resumed doggedly, "that it's a grandstand play. Redistricting has made you vulnerable for the first time. You've always depended on the conservative rural vote to send you to Washington, but now the more liberal urban voters of Masefield have to be wooed."

"What would you do in my position? Ignore them?"

The female aide hovered closer. For an instant Meg found herself wondering how a pretty young woman, maybe twenty-five to Meg's thirty, had already achieved a position of such responsibility. The woman possessed a wistful toughness, as if she didn't enjoy playing the heavy as often as her job required. With brown hair, brown eyes, and pale, translucent skin, she was pretty enough to be an adornment without being a distraction.

"But there's something else," Meg continued. "Some people say you've spent too much time in Washington and are out of touch with Illinois voters. They say you're more interested in becoming a national figure than in helping the people back home. So this move to a crumbling neighborhood and, no doubt, your walking tour today, are purely cosmetic. They enhance your image as 'the people's choice.' But in fact they say you have no intention of actually taking up residence here or of concerning yourself with the hard-core poverty issues, as your opponent, Ted Saunders, has done." She stopped, blood singing in her ears.

"'They' say all that, do 'they'? Tell me, do you know what a politician's fondest wish is, Ms. Birdsong? No? Then I'll tell you. It isn't to win a nomination or an election. It's to have five minutes alone in a locked room with 'they.'"

The aide stepped between them. "Sorry to cut this short, but you were due at City Hall ten minutes ago. Great pix with the kids, by the way. We'll use one in the newsletter. Let's run. Mrs. D. said—"

Delaney took the aide by the arm and moved her out of the way without looking at her. "Where do you live?" he asked Meg with sharpened interest.

"On Allston, about four blocks from here."

"Why? I know the street. It wouldn't be anybody's first choice."

"I can't afford to live anywhere else, among other reasons."

"Then it's my wealth that makes me suspect? The devious rich versus the honest poor? I'd expect a social worker to have a more sophisticated grasp of political reality." The smile again, to sugar-coat the pill.

Meg didn't smile. "I said there are other reasons. I have my constituents, too. I like living among the people I work with. I like city life. This neighborhood has a lot of character, and I don't want to see it turned into a parking lot."

"Those sound remarkably like my reasons. Why are they all right for you and not for me?"

Into the Whirlwind 11

Meg twisted her turquoise ring around and around while she searched for an answer. At the same time she noticed that although the playground was crowded, she and the congressman stood apart.

"Do you live alone?" he asked suddenly.

"Why do you want to know?"

"*Do* you?"

There was no mistaking the thrust of his question. Meg lifted her chin. "No, I don't."

The aide intervened once more. Mustn't let the congressman talk too long, Meg remarked to herself, or he might accidentally say something candid. In fact, he just had. Was this why Marcia Delaney had wanted him to leave? No doubt politicians had groupies just as rock stars did. Did Delaney take advantage of them?

He was turning away, looking for someone in his group.

So what if she angered him? Meg thought quickly, pushing their last exchange out of her mind. She would never have another chance to confront a U.S. Congressman with the grievances she heard every day from the children and families she counseled.

"Then tell me what difference your living here will actually make," she demanded in a louder voice. "Will you visit the housing project on Ninth? Can you find out why the federal funds to repair the plumbing have been tied up for two years? And what about the restrictions on funding shelters for runaways? Where do you stand on that? The place on Carlyle is going broke, and there's so much need for it. Then there's Ingersoll School—"

A reporter materialized beside them. "Can you give us a statement about the education bill, congressman?"

The PR people closed in. "Time's up. The congressman has another engagement."

To the group at large, which now included a sizable number of ordinary citizens, Delaney said in a practiced cadence, "The issues raised here are too complex to answer fully at this time; but I assure you all that I am committed to working for the people of Illinois, first and foremost. Problems brought to the notice of my offices, here or in Washington, will receive my personal attention as soon as possible."

His people formed a flying wedge around him, and Delaney moved off, shaking hands, tossing out greetings, patting heads.

From behind Meg, Jonathan squeezed her shoulders admiringly. "Congratulations. I didn't know you had it in you."

"Neither did I." She still tingled from Delaney's energy. Watching him depart was like watching a comet blaze away, leaving the sky darker than it had been before.

Over her shoulder, Jonathan teased, "What do you think? Are you impressed?"

Delaney was outside the fence now, still shaking hands and laughing.

"He's slick, all right," Meg replied. "You couldn't get a straight answer out of him with a crowbar."

"You mean you're not going to vote for him?"

"Of course not. We're miles apart on social issues. My issues."

"The charisma didn't work on you either, huh?"

She twitched her shoulders, and Jonathan took his hands away. Why was he needling her? "Did you hear my whole conversation with Delaney?"

They were opening the door of the big black car for the congressman.

"No," Jonathan answered. "I just heard the last part. Funniest thing. His people kept everyone from getting too close while the two of you were having it out. I guess they could see you were taking him to task, and they didn't want any negative publicity."

"I guess so." Or Delaney's people knew about his eye for the ladies and wanted to keep *that* out of the papers.

In the distance, Delaney was jackknifing his large frame into the car. Instinctively, Meg stood on tiptoes for a last look.

"Show's over," Jonathan was saying. "Back to the mines."

Just then, Cash Delaney stood up again and looked back over the playground. Sighting her, he raised an arm in farewell.

Meg waved back. With a grin he disappeared into the car. In thirty seconds, the car was out of sight. In sixty, the street had emptied.

At seven P.M., Jonathan met her at the door of his apartment with a glass of white wine and a chuckle. "Have you seen the evening paper?"

"No, I haven't had time. I had to take Jessie shopping for shoes after her gym class." She handed him the bakery strudel.

"There are two items that might interest you. First, this one." He tendered her an inside section. IRATE SCHOOL EMPLOYEE AND CONGRESSMAN IN CANDID EXCHANGE, the caption read. And there Meg was, mouth open, one hand raised, looking like a sparrow picking a fight with an eagle, while Cash Delaney regarded her with apparent concern and patience.

"You can read that article in a minute," Jonathan said. "It doesn't have much meat in it. But here's the scoop. They had to stop the presses to get this one into the evening edition." He handed over the front page.

DIVORCE REVEALED, the bulletin announced.

"Seems that Marcia Delaney obtained a quickie divorce before the primary," Jonathan explained, "but her father and the Delaney camp convinced her to hold off on announcing it until after the election. She's a good speaker, a real asset, and her family guarantees Delaney's ties to the political power structure. But this week she decided she'd had enough and leaked word to the press so he'd have to let her go. It's ironic."

"What's ironic?" Meg sat down on the couch, the words of the article swimming on the page.

"Delaney's buying that town house in darkest downtown Masefield seems to have been the last straw. Mrs. Delaney likes the Washington scene, and she also likes the resort life with their wealthy friends. She wasn't about to get to know the great unwashed that put her husband in office. She seems to think, in fact, that he's starting to take his job too seriously. Would you like a cheese straw?" Jonathan went to the kitchen. "We witnessed an historic occasion," he called cheerily. "The last public appearance of the Delaneys as man and wife. Though, of course, they were already divorced."

Meg felt a sickening rush of exhilaration, as if she were falling to her destruction through beautiful sunlit clouds. Then she just felt sick. What a cold so-and-so to let his wife walk away without turning a hair. But maybe he had been expecting it. Of course he had. He had been forcing her to stay with him, for his own gain. Meg felt the old tension tighten her shoulders. She knew what it was like to live with someone side by side, day after day, after the love had gone. She knew how deep you had to dig to find the courage to say, *Enough*. Poor Marcia Delaney. Meg smoothed the newspaper over her lap and stared at the floor, seeing again Delaney asking, "Do you live alone?" It had been brash, all right, but he had been free to ask. If only she had explained her situation to him...

"Earth to Meg, earth to Meg." Jonathan leaned around the door. "Come in, Meg."

Obediently, she went to join him, thinking to herself that her neighbor Ruth was right. Meg had the it's-later-than-you-think divorcée blues, in which any man this side of Howdy Doody looks like a real romantic possibility. If Cash Delaney was so ambitious, then he wouldn't waste time on a political nonentity like herself, especially one who disagreed with him on every major issue. He had only been making conversation with a face in the crowd.

"I think I will have a cheese straw," she announced, and took one.

But she didn't taste it.

CHAPTER TWO

"SWEET DREAMS." MEG pulled up Jessie's sheet and kissed her forehead.

"Can't you read one more chapter of *Hitty?*"

"Not tonight." Meg flipped off the overhead light. "Doughnuts for breakfast."

"Oh, boy..." Jessie curled around her teddy bear, eyes already closing.

In the living room, the rusty window fan railed hopelessly against the heat. Meg switched on the radio and the frosted, sensual dream of Chopin's *Concerto No. 1 in E Minor* trickled out. She hesitated between the stack of library books on the coffee table and the counted cross-stitch project lying in the willow chair. School had been out for a week, and she was still adjusting to freedom. Finally, she knelt at the window overlooking Allston Street, four floors below, to let the faint breeze ice down the sunburn she'd gotten at the community pool.

In the window of the building across the street, a

woman in a housedress paused in her ironing to wipe her sweaty face with a forearm. Under the streetlight on the corner, several half-grown kids played kick-the-can. A police cruiser slid by, looking for trouble. Someone gunned a motorcycle in the alley, and exhaust fumes surged up. Behind her, Chopin whispered of drawing rooms hung with green silk, of sauternes in crystal goblets, of long, pale hands caressing Cattleya orchids. Though it hadn't always been that way, she belonged to the street now. She'd choose it over Chopin every time. What the hell, you could still see the moon from it.

Someone knocked at the door.

It was probably Ruth wanting to chat, which meant that Tom was working late again. Yawning, Meg went to the door and opened it.

Cash Delaney straightened from leaning against the doorjamb and asked, "What do you mean, you don't live alone?"

He wore a light blue shirt, regimental-striped tie, gray slacks and cordovan loafers. A navy sports jacket lay across a briefcase on the floor beside him. "I just got into town. I had the taxi drop me here."

Astonishment, like a sonic boom, finally hit her. "Are you . . . campaigning door-to-door?"

"Just at your door. It's good to see you again, Meg."

He was seeing her, all right. His eyes roved from the top of her head, where her hair was loosely held up with tortoise-shell combs, touched on her face and the gold chain at her neck, lingered on her shirred pink tube top, which rolled her breasts together melonlike, moved slowly over the faded cutoffs that she had hacked off at the edge of her panties, and down her firm, sunblushed legs to her bare feet.

"May I come in?"

"Oh yes, please, I'm sorry." She moved aside.

He crossed the threshold, glanced around, and cocked an eyebrow at her. "Well?"

"Right this way, congressman." She led him down the hall to Jessie's doorway. Jessie was now sleeping on her back, pigtails awry. "That's my roommate," Meg whispered. "Jessie. She's been with me just over a year."

"Adopted?"

"No, she's my foster daughter."

"There's just the two of you, then?"

"That's right."

In the narrow doorway, Delaney took her by the shoulders and turned her to face him. He smiled slowly. "This makes things a lot easier." His thumb stroked the tiny tattooed rosebud on her left shoulder. In Meg's mind, the bud softened, unfurled...

"Congressman."

"Cash."

"That's just my point." She looked into his eyes, and something convulsed sharply inside her, like hunger. "What is this all about? We don't even know each other."

"I want us to get to know each other. How about going out for a drink? I'll bet there's a nice neighborhood bar or restaurant within walking distance."

"Yes, but..." She ducked out from under his hands and headed for the living room.

"A certain pretty lady once accused me of not taking an interest in Masefield," he said at her shoulder. "This is her chance to show me around."

"But there's Jessie."

"Wake her up. We'll take her with us."

Meg drifted to a halt in the middle of the living room. Chopin's crystal palace had been knocked down to make room for one of Bach's airy, brass cages. Behind her, Delaney walked over to the bookcase. She wanted to go out with him, of course. It was his steamroller tactics that called up her resistance. That and the simple shock of his having remembered her.

"What's this?" He was examining one of the flyers from the open box on the bookcase. "Campaign literature for Ted Saunders? You work for my opponent?"

"Ye-es, in a way. That is, Jonathan is pretty heavily involved in Ted's campaign, and I agreed to stuff envelopes."

His stare nailed her to the wall. "Jonathan?"

"A friend. You met him at Ingersoll School, remember?"

"No I don't." He tossed the flyer back in the box and loosed his million-dollar smile at her. "I was too busy looking at you."

Meg looked at her toes.

"You voted against me in the primary, didn't you?"

"Yes."

"And also the three other times I ran for Congress?"

"Yes."

"Well, then." Delaney sat on the arm of the couch and folded his arms. "I'm going to convince you of the error of your ways, madam, if it takes all night. Shall we go out or stay here?"

Smiling, she threw up her hands. "I'll just go and change."

Five minutes later she was back, wearing her handmade sandals, charcoal cotton slacks, a pale gray linen jacket over the tube top, and hoop earrings of beaten silver.

"That didn't take long. You must not be vain," he greeted her.

"I guess not."

"You should be."

She called Ruth and asked her to look in on Jessie.

When they went out, Delaney left his briefcase behind.

The Fern Bar, three blocks away, more than lived up to its name. Hanging baskets of greenery turned the light dim and feathery, and the air was as cool as a forest glade. They took a secluded corner table, under a massive Swedish ivy. While Delaney ordered Mexican beer and a plate of deep-fried mushrooms to share, Meg thought of how Ruth had looked when she'd opened her door and seen Delaney standing behind Meg in the hall. Surely by now Ruth had gotten her jaw up off the floor.

Meg explained, "This place was a soda fountain from the forties until the sixties, but then it was abandoned for a long time. About a year and a half ago, a couple from Chicago bought it. You can see they've preserved the original counter—I think it's walnut—and the black-and-white floor tiles. They won some kind of award for the renovation, and—"

He touched her hand. "Tell me about yourself."

"I thought you wanted to know about the neighborhood."

"I can ask my neighbors."

The waitress set down a round black tray and unloaded cocktail napkins, glasses, and bottles. She opened the beers and filled the glasses. Delaney paid her, and she went off swishing her black taffeta skirt and eyeing Delaney over her shoulder.

Meg propped her elbows on the table and rested her chin on the palms of her hands. "Do you do this often?"

"Do what?"

"Pick somebody out of the crowd to dazzle."

He drank as if he'd been thinking about a drink for a long time. "Not often. Do you know why I picked you?"

"Tell me."

"Because you struck me as the kind of woman who just might decide to spend some time with me without regard to my press releases."

Meg watched a bead of moisture trickle down her glass. "I'm being awful. I'm sorry."

"Why did you agree to come here if that's the way you feel?"

"I don't know. I can't pretend that I'm not affected by your reputation. Maybe I wanted to see if there's anything behind it."

"There is. So you don't scare me."

She began to draw with her finger in the condensation on the glass. "You mean you don't use it?"

"Use what?"

"Your reputation, your status—as a lever to get what you want in personal relationships."

"Give me an example."

She saw that she had drawn a heart. "When you showed up at my door tonight, you were absolutely certain I wouldn't refuse to see you, no matter what my plans or situation might be. And you moved so fast, as if... as if you knew you had an edge... as if you'd never been refused."

Her left hand lay spread on the table. Delaney began to trace the veins of her hand with an index finger. "That has nothing to do with being a congressman. I've always moved fast. When I see something I want, that is."

She swallowed and glanced up at a cool smile and hot eyes.

Abruptly, he laughed. "I could use someone like you on my staff, Meg. You're a natural-born devil's advocate. You ask some tough questions."

"I don't mean to. It's just that I'm..." She didn't know what she was.

"Careful. I'm careful, too. So tell me about yourself."

They both laughed.

The mushrooms arrived.

For no good reason, she began to relax. "I'm originally from Indiana. I came to Masefield to go to college, majoring in French. Back then, I went to Europe as often as possible, bumming around from one student hostel to another, and even lived in Grenoble for a year. But the summer after I graduated, I got a job here in town at the residence program for emotionally disturbed children. It woke me up. I found that I wanted to help people, at a basic level, where so-called high culture can't reach. Doesn't mean beans. Put studying neo-Marxist theories of literature up against bringing an autistic child even one step out of his shadowy world and see what choice *you* make." She nibbled a mushroom and took a sip of beer. "Anyway, I went back to school for training in social work. I get frustrated sometimes, but I've never regretted my decision."

"And your personal life?"

"I was married for a while. It didn't work out. Everybody's fault and nobody's."

"No children?"

"One of the worst ways to try to save a marriage is to have a child. I realized that just in time."

"But you wanted children. Hence, Jessie."

"I guess so. But I really took Jessie for a different reason." She frowned, ordering her words. "I started out in this profession thinking that I could save the world. As time went on and I saw how many people need help and realized how very difficult it is to reach some people no matter how hard you try, I revised my ambitions. The best I could do, the only realistic goal, was to help one person at a time."

"Mother Teresa says that."

"I'm no saint. I just found a little kid who needed a place to go."

The waitress took Delaney's order for a refill. When she brought it, she squirmed and asked, "Could you autograph this napkin? And one for my friend over there?"

Taking the pen from her, he gave her a grin that would keep her warm for a week. After the waitress left, he said to Meg, "Tell me more."

"I don't know why I've told you as much as I have. You must be a good listener. Have you ever thought of social work?"

"There may not be as much difference between our two jobs as you think."

"Tell me about your job. Your life. Something that isn't in the press releases."

"But they're all true," he said winningly. It gave her the idea he wasn't going to be sincere.

"Why did you go into politics?" she pressed. "I've never read anything about that."

"To help people. To make a difference. Your goal, but a different method. And on a grander scale." He was watching her more carefully now. "Of course I like the recognition, and the glamour too. Who wouldn't? But I work hard for it."

"A servant of the people?"

"That's right." His eyes narrowed.

"But what gave you the idea? You've led such a privileged life: a well-to-do upbringing, private eastern education, going straight from Law Review into a lucrative practice, ready-made political contacts provided by your father-in-law."

"A man doesn't have to get his foot blown off to know that war is hell," he snapped. "Cut the poorer-and-holier-than-thou business."

"I just wanted to know... I didn't mean to suggest that you're insensitive or that you don't deserve the success you've had."

"Didn't you?" His voice was a blunt instrument.

Her heart thudded nauseatingly. Why hadn't she realized what she was saying? It was the remark about his father-in-law that had gotten to him. A reporter had once asked Delaney if he'd ridden into Congress on Sam DeWitt's coattails. Delaney had punched his lights out.

Meg rolled her glass between her palms and tried to make her voice light. "One of my job skills is asking questions, you know. Lots of times I get answers out of people without their even knowing I'm asking. But I'm not doing a very good job with you, am I?"

"Maybe it's because you think you already have all the answers," he returned coldly.

But something drove her on. "I read about your divorce."

"So did I," he cracked.

She kept fooling with her glass. It gave her something to look at.

"People who say I married purely for political gain are having a hard time explaining a divorce in the middle of the toughest campaign of my career," he noted.

Recalling the scene on the playground, Meg wondered if Marcia Delaney was a blackmailer. What might she have demanded in exchange for staying with her husband, say at least until after the election? Meg studied the congressman with a series of up-from-under glances. Had his cool calling of Marcia's bluff cost him more than a wife? Campaign funds? Endorsements? Maybe Cash Delaney had courage. Sam DeWitt wouldn't like to see his only daughter pushed around.

"Like to let me in on the conversation?" Delaney slouched in his chair, one arm thrown over the back.

"I was trying to think of something funny to say."

"I'll bet you were." A long minute passed. They drank, listened to the piped-in music. Abruptly, he said, "It's good to talk to you. Thanks for coming along."

She gaped at him. "But I'm saying all the wrong things."

"Not at all. It's been a long time since I've talked to someone who doesn't want anything out of me and who isn't trying to impress me."

"Don't you have any friends?"

"See there? You're doing it again. Rushing in where angels fear to tread. It's refreshing. Of course I have friends. I just don't have enough time for them."

"You ought to do something about that."

"I am." He took her hand. "I'd like to make a friend of you. And more. Of course honesty isn't everything. There's also the fact that you're a knockout woman."

Her hand trembled in his. "To be honest with you, it won't work."

"Why not?"

"This whole evening is wrong. We live in different worlds, can't you see that? You live on jets, in heated swimming pools. You spend weekends at Vail or Aspen with the rich and powerful. My life is a fourth-floor walk-up, abused children, families on welfare."

"'Give me your tired, your poor...' You're making yourself sound like the Statue of Liberty."

She colored. "Your values are not my values."

"I'm only talking about getting to know each other, not a lifelong commitment," he observed sarcastically. "Don't you have any curiosity about how the other half lives?"

"I'm just a novelty to you."

"In a way. I've certainly never met anyone like you."

He had the blarney to go with his Irish name. She started to speak, but he beat her to it.

"Meg, do you ever have any fun?"

She wasn't expecting that. "Of course I do."

"I wonder. You seem to take life so seriously. You know, denying yourself small pleasures, maybe a little adventure, isn't going to help your clients any."

His words cut deep, deeper than she would ever let him know. What could he know of sacrifice, of loneliness? Sensing that he wouldn't let her change the subject, she went on to the next step. She pulled her hand away from his and picked up her purse. "I need to be getting home."

"I'm not criticizing you," he said with the expected stubborness. "I'm just asking if you're as happy as you could be."

"I really must go. Jessie might wake up."

"A convenient excuse."

"Jessie was once abandoned by her mother in a bus station. She has fears other people don't have. If she wakes up and I'm not there, she could go into hysterics." Meg stood up.

The light of interest went out of his eyes. He tossed a bill on the table. "You win. Let's go."

It was true about Jessie, but Meg knew she had pushed him too far. Damn, she fretted as they left the restaurant. She hadn't been this inept since her first date. And yet, hadn't he started the pushing? Her happiness was none of his business!

Outside the bar, the night air was as heavy and moist as an unwanted kiss.

Meg pointed across the street. "We can cut through Trelawney Park."

He offered his arm with an ironic flourish.

She took it and went on kicking herself mentally.

But somehow, in spite of everything, it felt right to let him guide her steps. They took a winding path lit by old-fashioned globe lights, past a bird bath, a statue of an Indian mother and child, a fountain, a couple entwined on a park bench. The breeze brought the sour velvet odor of petunias, a whisper of leaf mold and evergreens, the sugary aroma of fresh-cut grass and, underneath all that, the gray chemical odor of the city. They slowed to a stroll. They didn't speak. That felt right, too. A man you could be comfortably silent with was rare. She wouldn't have expected Cash Delaney to be one of them. They moved together to let a cyclist pass, and there were soft collisions of their shoulders, hips, her arm against his ribs. Her hand clenched on his sleeve as desire flooded her.

"What's wrong?"

"Nothing."

They came out of the park on Allston Street, half a block from her apartment building.

"How long will you be in town?" she asked, trying to sound merely polite.

"I'm holding a hearing here until noon tomorrow. The rest of the weekend I'll be campaigning elsewhere in the district. I have to be back in Washington by Sunday night. Tonight was the only time I could see you."

He sounded cordial again. Maybe she hadn't completely blown the evening. Awkwardly, she offered, "I'm glad you came by, although I don't know why."

"Don't know why I came, or don't know why you're glad?"

"Both." They climbed the steps of 910 Allston. She reached for the door.

His hand came down over hers on the knob. "I have the answer to both questions."

Staring into the dark, handsome face bent expectantly over hers, she forgot to speak, think, breathe...

"Evening, folks." Old Mr. Morris from the first floor toiled up the steps with his dog, Brandy. They stood aside to let him enter. Then it was time to say good-bye. If she'd meant what she'd said earlier, this was the place for a nice, clean break.

"Would you like to come in?" she asked. "I mean, anyway, your briefcase—"

"Yes."

She led him to the stairs.

He was playing her like a fish on a line, she thought. It was scary. Jonathan always let her know what he was thinking and feeling, so that she could decide on her own position. It was part of his personality to do so, as well as part of his training in counseling. Jonathan was courteous, kind, and sensitive to her needs. He treated her with the respect due an equal. But this man, whose eyes even now she could feel caressing her back, rear, and legs as he climbed after her, this man didn't give a hoot about her needs or about equality. He wanted to dominate. He wanted whatever he wanted, and without any explanations to her. She was a fool to encourage him. But she wasn't ready to say good-bye.

By the time they got to her floor, even though she

was used to the stairs, she was panting and perspiring. Delaney came up beside her, not winded. She dropped her keys twice before she got the door open.

"I'll just tell Ruth I'm home. Make yourself comfortable."

"I will." He sauntered in.

As Meg raised her hand to knock on Ruth's door, it opened.

"Not a peep out of Jessie," Ruth whispered. "Tell: what, how, where, when, and why."

"I don't have any answers, Ruthie. I appreciate your watching Jessie."

"Are you okay? You look like you're coming down with something."

"I think maybe I am," Meg said. "Good night."

Delaney was at a living room window, watching the street. He had removed his jacket and unknotted his tie.

Meg looked in on Jessie, then came back to the living room and turned on the window fan.

Now what? she thought. "It's so hot in here. I'll get some ice water."

He grinned at her over his shoulder. She was just a happy little rainbow trout, running with the line. The grin told her he knew exactly when to reel her in.

The kitchen was a tight U-shaped space off the living room, so small that she could mop the floor with one paper towel. She got out a tray of ice and ran water over it. She took two glasses from the cabinet, put three ice cubes in each, and filled them with water from the tap. She put the ice tray back in the freezer and dried her shaking hands.

"You'd be cooler with that jacket off." His hands were on her shoulders, peeling the jacket down.

She spun around and was in his arms, staring at his sensuous mouth, a mouth to make women weep. Her jacket slid to the floor.

She asked, "Why did you come here? Don't expect me to believe you simply picked me out of the crowd because of my looks or my personality. You've seen too many crowds."

"Can you think of another reason?"

"No."

"Then believe it." He gathered her closer.

"What do you *really* want?"

"Everything you're imagining I want. But I'm not in as big a hurry as you think."

She backed away, but the counter stopped her before she got out of his embrace. "I suppose you never have to wait long, do you? They just fall into your arms and into your bed, don't they? All those women who are thrilled to be noticed by a congressman?"

"Nothing worth having is that easy to get."

"But you take it anyway."

"No I don't. Sorry to disappoint you, but I'm an ethical man. I was a faithful husband."

Ice shifted in a glass. The counter cut into her hip. Her eyes dropped to a button on his shirt. "I'm sorry. Again. I don't know what's the matter with me tonight."

Delaney's thumb circled slowly on the bare skin between her shoulder blades. "Don't apologize. I like your fight. You're a strong woman, and I find that a challenge. But you're also bendable. In fact, I think you've been looking for someone to make you bend, whether consciously or not."

Her pulse fluttered. "And you think you can do it?"

"It would be my pleasure. You and I could give each other a great deal of pleasure, Meg."

He pulled her against him by the waist, so that her back arched and her head fell back, her lips softening with helpless hunger to meet his. She gripped handfuls of his shirt as pure sensation dissolved her into him, so that she felt her feelings and his, somehow shared the questing pressure of his body from inside him, felt his irresistible will hammering at her most secret defenses. She sighed, drowning in the heat of his mouth and the sinking, terrible joy of her heart.

"You see? A great deal of pleasure," he murmured, continuing to explore her mouth.

"This is happening too fast... please... it's like..."

"Like what?" He kissed just below her ear.

"I don't know. We've cut through... all the preliminaries. It's like walking in the front door of a building and finding yourself on the top floor."

"And how do you like my penthouse?"

"Please, Cash. You'd better go."

"Leave? Now that we're finally on a first-name basis?"

She started to twist out of his arms, but the way her whole body responded to the next kiss made a liar out of her. When it was over she sagged against him; everything to her knees was an erogenous zone.

"Rubberbanding," he said, stroking her back.

"What?"

"Isn't that what they call it in your profession? This advance-and-retreat behavior you're exhibiting? You've been doing it all night."

"Can you blame me for being confused? You're not—" She bit her lip. Not Jonathan, who would never put this kind of pressure on her. The pool of heat Cash's fingers made on her back was spreading a liquid yearning through her veins. Desperately, she pulled away from him and wrapped her arms tightly about herself. Behind her, silence. She looked back.

Delaney was looking at the wall clock. "It's late." He visibly cooled. "When can I see you again?"

Surely he didn't have another appointment at this hour, she thought in confusion. "I'm sure you're very busy."

The haze of preoccupation in his eyes cleared. "I'll find the time. Can you?"

She went back to the living room. But there was no use running away. Besides, she didn't want to. She faced him. "Yes, I can find the time. When?"

Cash slung his coat over his arm and picked up his briefcase. Like a magician pulling a bouquet out of a hat, he produced The Smile. "I'll call you."

Don't call us, we'll call you, she jeered silently. He'd decided to cut his losses. She walked stiffly to the door and opened it for him. "Thank you for stopping by."

He halted in front of her and scrutinized her face. Mysterious lights played far back in his eyes, like summer lightning in the mountains.

A door was opened and shut down the hall, letting out a burst of radio music. In that moment, Meg felt the weakening connection between them snap.

Delaney felt it too. He lifted a hand, as if to touch her cheek, and let it fall. "Good night, Meg."

"Good night." She closed the door after him.

She wandered back to the kitchen and looked at the clock. What had it reminded him of? She poured the ice water down the sink, dried the glasses, returned them to the cabinet, and wiped the rings off the counter.

The telephone at her elbow jangled.

"Hello?"

"Is Congressman Delaney there? This is Brenda Garrison."

"No, he just left. You can probably reach him at home in a few minutes."

"That's where I'm calling from. Okay, thanks." The lines went dead.

Brenda Garrison, the attractive aide, must have flown in from Washington with him that evening. What sort of relationship did they have? Had she been waiting all this time for him to return from Meg's? Would anyone wait that long out of professional loyalty? Meg hung up the receiver. So that was why he had left so abruptly. He had a more willing partner waiting at home.

She hurried to the living room window. She could just make out a tall figure turning the corner two blocks away. The only place she ever wanted to see Congressman Cash Delaney again was on the evening news. A man like that could break her heart without even noticing. She had spent only one evening with him, and she could already feel it cracking.

CHAPTER THREE

FOG SWATHED TRELAWNEY PARK. A white patch low in the general grayness marked the position of the rising sun. Passing the mile post on the jogging path for the second time, Meg watched two squirrels spiral down the trunk of an elm, and she imagined that the fog was magic and that it made her invisible. Sunday stretched before her like a silent, glassy lake. She cruised around a boy walking a schnauzer. Somewhere in the fog two men conversed disjointedly, and she pictured the park statues talking to each other. She began to plan her day. What looked better with every step was a shower, followed by a return to bed with coffee and the Sunday paper. Later she would repot plants and bake bread, before it was time to go to the matinee with Jonathan. She leaped a pothole and slowed to a more comfortable pace. She was at peace.

The peace lasted until she noticed that the two male voices that had been coming from her left were now somewhere on the jogging path behind her. Trelawney Park was safe; but she stopped feeling invisible. She glanced back and saw a sea of fog. The voices had stopped. She went back to planning. After the matinee, she and Jonathan would pick up Jessie, and they'd all go out for hamburgers. Then...

The voices again, very near. Unworried but cautious, she accelerated mildly. Suddenly, she heard one set of footsteps bounding after her. She turned—

"Is it safe for you to run alone at this hour?" Cash drifted alongside her.

For several moments she panted in silence while her heart slowed its fearful pounding. "It has been up until now."

"I disagree. You need an escort." Pointedly, he eyed her cotton turtleneck and skimpy running shorts. Cash himself looked handsomer and larger than ever in an old gray sweatsuit, with his hair tousled and his eyes crackling with energy. "I tried to call you last night from Williamstown. I was giving a speech there."

"I took Jessie to visit her family. She stayed overnight." She was glad they were moving; one good look at her face would tell him how happy she was to see him again.

They looped around the playground. Cash jerked a thumb backward. "That's Roger back there. My press secretary. This was the only time today we could talk."

Meg waved to a stocky, red-faced young man some yards behind. Innocently, she said, "I suppose you got in touch with Brenda Garrison Friday night. She called just after you left."

"Yes I did."

"Do you ever do anything without an aide, Congressman?"

"That depends on how fast you can run."

"Oh? And where are we running to?"

"To your place. I've inviting myself to breakfast."

Ten minutes later, Meg extracted the door key from her zippered wristband and let them into the apartment.

"*Now* I'll have that glass of ice water." Cash followed her into the kitchen.

Beneath the glow of exercise, Meg felt herself blush. She tossed him a hand towel and blotted her face on a second one, the casual actions masking her nervous exhilaration. "After you left, I thought I had dreamed your visit. This one isn't much more real."

"When is it going to get real? By next time?"

Avoiding his eyes, she handed him a glass of water. "Will there be a next time?"

His vitality charged the air with an almost unbearable tension, of which he appeared to be unaware. He downed the water and set aside the glass. "Do you always answer a question with a question?" He stepped around her and opened the refrigerator. "Let's see. How about a cheese omelet?"

"*You're* fixing breakfast?"

He lifted her easily by the waist and set her on the counter. "Yes. Do you mind?"

"No..." Because his hands were still warm on her waist, and he was standing between her knees and his lips were so close.... He kissed her softly, tentatively, and then again with a quiet force that penetrated her to the center of feeling. The next thing she knew, her arms were around his neck, and she was whispering against his cheek, "You can fix my breakfast anytime."

"We ought to start the night before and work up to breakfast, don't you think?"

Her answer was the way she responded to the next kiss. Mildly scandalized at herself, she realized that she couldn't hide anything from him. She wanted him to know how much he excited her; and admitting it excited her even more. Nobody had ever made her act like this.

It was Cash who had to break it up. He detached her arms from his neck and kissed the backs of her hands.

"You heard what Roger shouted as we sprinted away. I have four appearances to make today, one of them seventy miles away." He turned back to the refrigerator.

In a daze, Meg watched him work, directing him to utensils when he asked. It was endearing to observe him whistling, dropping and spilling things, throwing out a quip now and then. He was like a boy playing hooky. She sipped water. Was that her appeal for him? Her low-keyed, totally unglamorous life? Was it possible that here he could be himself, a self few people ever saw? Or was she just fooling herself? Why should he let his guard down for her? Maybe there was no such thing as the private Cash Delaney. Maybe you could take the boy out of the limelight, but never the limelight out of the boy. Yet while Cash grated cheese and beat eggs, she let herself dream that she might have something important to offer him: a secret place away from publicity and decision-making. He had been in the news since his high school athletic days and often actively sought exposure; but the glare of public scrutiny must get tiring. And she would ask nothing in return except to know him, really know him. That, she was beginning to realize, she wanted badly.

"Do you do a lot of cooking?" she asked.

"Hell, no." He flung down a hot spatula and knocked over the salt with his elbow. "Marcia and I had a cook. Eggs and coffee is my entire repertoire." He blew on his fingers, then put the burn out of his mind and began to measure coffee into the coffee maker. He winked at her. "But I've just figured out what the kitchen in my town house needs: a good-looking, hungry woman perched on the counter. That could inspire me."

Marcia. How could she have forgotten Marcia? Perhaps her own appeal was nothing more than her availability. He was newly divorced. Meg remembered the sudden craving to connect with people again after the pain had subsided. The first connections were invariably mistakes. She slid off the counter. "I'll set the table."

The table was around the corner, in the living room. After she had set it, she wandered to the window, shucking off her turtleneck. The fog was burning off fast, leaving the humidity high.

Cash came in with two plates of eggs and toast. He nodded at her T-shirt. "You really believe that?"

She had forgotten she was wearing the one that said A WOMAN NEEDS A MAN LIKE A FISH NEEDS A BICYCLE. "A friend gave it to me the day my divorce became final. I tried to believe it for a while. It may be true. But I happen to be a fish who likes bicycles."

He grinned. "Welcome to the Tour de France."

When they sat down, Meg moved the Sunday paper from her chair and an item caught her eye. "That 'Where the Action Is' column is about your campaign stops yesterday."

"Yes, I remember the reporter." He poured coffee for both of them as Meg skimmed the account. It covered the hearing in Masefield, a luncheon with senior citizens, a clinic opening out in the county, a dinner speech. The article was frankly admiring, as she would have expected; the *Masefield Gazette* endorsed Delaney down the line.

"Hey. I said, How do you like breakfast?" he demanded.

"Fine, it's fine."

"How could you possibly know?"

"I'm sorry." She laid the paper aside and tasted the eggs. "Why, they're really good!"

Her disbelief made him chuckle. "Now you owe me a meal."

Her attention strayed back to the article.

Abruptly, the newspaper was jerked away. "It would seem more logical to talk to me now and read about me later, when I'm not here," he observed.

The ego of the public figure, she noted fleetingly. "Williamstown. You tried to call me from Williamstown?"

"That's right."

"Sam DeWitt's farm is near there, isn't it?"

"True. I went to see him. Sam has a lot of pull, and he's still interested in my campaign."

She tried the coffee. It was strong enough to corrode steel. "The article says that Mar—that your wife—, I mean, that your ex-wife was also visiting."

His head snapped up.

Meg retrieved the paper and read, "'Informed sources say that Delaney, who did not contest the divorce, still hopes for a reconciliation. Marcia DeWitt, who has taken back her maiden name, is thought to be in seclusion at the DeWitt farm, but she was unavailable for comment.'"

"Give me that." As he read, the lines running from the edges of his nostrils to the corners of his mouth deepened and sharpened. He tossed the paper aside. "Damned hype. Do they think I'm a fool?"

Meg went to the kitchen for strawberry jam. She set it on the table and resumed her seat.

His jaw worked. "Getting married to Marcia was the single most selfish action of my life. I'm not a man to make the same mistake twice."

She buttered a piece of toast, halved it diagonally, and nibbled one of the points.

"It took me a while to realize what I'd done," he ground out. "When I did, I moved to end it."

She put down the toast, wiped her fingers on a napkin, and waited.

Finally, in a low, controlled voice, Cash said, "Marcia was better known in the state than I was when I entered politics: the witty, golden daughter of a gilt-edged dynasty. The Illinois equivalent of Alice Roosevelt Longworth. I thought I loved her, Meg, I did. But what I really loved was the life she was part of, the life of politics and power. I married her for what she represented, not for who she was inside. Power, or the nearness to power, gives people a shine like nothing else, no matter how reasonable you try to be about it." He stared at the tabletop. "It was an honest mistake—and yet it wasn't. I married her for the right reason—and yet I didn't."

"What about her?" Meg asked. "Did—does—she love you? Has she been hurt?"

"Marcia hurt?" He was silent for a minute. "I had the illusion of being in love. She didn't even have that, as it turned out. She expected me to carry her straight to the top. She'd like to be First Lady, of the state if not of the country. She'd be a good one, too." Again an edgy silence. "I let her get the divorce instead of me. That was one of her terms. But it was a mutual decision. I wasn't the perfect husband." After a moment, he added, "For her."

"But she stayed on."

He snorted. "Our marriage was over a long time ago. That was one of the best-kept secrets in Washington. Marcia and I have little in common besides ambition. But my father-in-law is a tough old bird who also happens to think I'm going places, with or without his daughter. His information indicated that a divorce during the campaign would damage my image with the voters. He persuaded us to preserve appearances for a time. Public office can be a seductive, corrupting prize if you want it too much. But lately I've remembered where my values are. Nothing is worth living that kind of lie." He jabbed the newspaper with a forefinger. "But the press—the press friendly to me—is going to keep our story running like a soap opera. Will we or won't we reconcile? Tune in tomorrow. And what does that have to do with the issues?"

"Nothing."

"That's exactly right." He hit the table with his fist. "She isn't at the farm. Sam doesn't know where she is. Neither do I. Nor do I care."

"You sound pretty disgusted," Meg said in a small voice.

He poured himself more coffee. "I generally don't let things get to me like this. It's been a long week." Meg watched something else replace his anger: a suspicious reserve, as if he suspected she had somehow tricked him into talking. "Enough about that," he said shortly.

They made the smallest of small talk until a clamor of chuch bells startled them.

Meg jumped out of her chair. "You'll be late."

"Relax. I'll make a phone call."

She had cleared the table and was curled on the couch, trying to concentrate on the Sunday comics, when he finished his call.

He sat down and threw an arm around her. "I'll shower and change in Taylor before my speech. Roger'll stop for my clothes on the way here. So we have a few minutes." They stared at each other. He spread a hand on her bare thigh. "I wish there was more time."

She licked her lips. "So do I."

"I like a woman who says what she's thinking." His hand moved up.

"Around you, I can't help it." Flame flickered between her legs.

"Good. That's the effect I was aiming for." He kissed her with teasing slowness. "It's good that you don't play games with me. We don't have time for it."

"Not this morning."

"I mean not ever." He kissed her again. Before she knew what was happening, she was lying on her back and he was settling himself over her, his chest brushing her breasts. "I'm thirty-eight years old. I know what I want and what I don't. And so do you." He searched her face. "Yes, so do you. So don't pretend otherwise."

She spread her legs to let him lie comfortably between them. His mouth, nuzzling the hollow of her throat and between her breasts, turned her wet and spongy inside. It was so easy just to let him, to help him...

Suddenly, she was on the verge of tears. She struggled to sit up. "Cash, this is crazy. What are we doing? Just what *do* you want? Five minutes of sex whenever you happen to be in the neighborhood? Do you have women stashed all along the campaign trail?"

He propped himself on an elbow. "Why did you get divorced?"

"The biggest reason? There was another woman."

"I thought so. Don't punish *me* for it. All I want is you." He went back to her trembling body, kissing her lips into tender, swelling moistness, fondling her breasts, caressing her lower and lower. She arched up against him, gripping his shoulders, and he paused with a wickedly tender twinkle in his eye. Stroking her nipples through her shirt with the flat of his palm, making them harden until she caught her lower lip in her teeth to keep from crying out, he observed, "At least your body doesn't lie."

"Damn you, do I have to shout it? Yes, you're a gorgeous, sexy man. Yes, you're driving me mad with wanting you. But you're also infuriating!"

He shifted purposefully, and she felt his arousal. "How's that?"

"You're so—so haughty, so sure of yourself!" She wiped her eyes angrily. "You think you can stalk into my life whenever you please and just take over!"

"Do you think I can help myself, witch? I wasn't looking for a relationship when I met you. With all this uproar over the divorce, it's the last thing I need. We'd better hope a reporter doesn't—"

"Oh!" She struck at him. With a metallic laugh, he caught her wrist, ducked as she hit out with her other hand, and caught that one too. Kicking and scuffling, she managed to sit up. When he unexpectedly released her, she bounced off the couch and hit the floor on her tailbone. She scrambled to her feet. "Excuse me for being so politically inconvenient!"

"I didn't mean that." Still laughing, he came after her.

"Get away." She backed off. Out of habit, she glanced out the window. "Your car's here."

Cash opened the window screen, leaned out, and motioned to the driver. Then he straightened and considered her coolly. "Every time I see you, I want to see more of you. If you want to be stubborn about this, go ahead. I can be stubborn, too. It isn't going to end here and now."

It flashed through her mind that they were fighting like people who had a stake in each other's lives. Her anger stumbled. She turned sharply away. Haltingly, she said, "The worst part is, I like the way you take over, every bit as much as I resent it. Somehow I need it. And... it turns me on."

He put an arm around her and drew her head down on his chest. "We're quite a match, you and I. My guess is you've never met a man who could come close to handling you. Until now."

Arrogant to the last. She sighed. All the same, he was leaving. And even if she somehow managed to keep his interest on his trips to Masefield, everything would change after the election. His political instincts would reassert themselves, and he wouldn't have time for her. He'd be one of Washington's most eligible bachelors. He'd be looking for another high-profile companion.

"Come to Washington," he said.

"What?"

"For a weekend. Soon." He tilted her chin up.

She hesitated. It was a hard decision, but she had to make it. "I don't think so."

"Why not?"

Yes, why not? Because—because now she remembered once again who he was and what his life was like.

It was so easy to forget that when she was in his arms.

"Next weekend." He ran a thumb along her jaw. "Uninterrupted time together in the most interesting city in the world. We might even see some of it."

"Some of Washington?"

"Sure we might. After we've gotten to know each other a lot better. And speaking of what I want, you and I both know that sex is very easy to come by, if that's all you're looking for."

"Speak for yourself."

"No smart remarks. You know what I'm talking about. I want us to know everything about each other. At the risk of sounding corny, hearts and minds too."

But this morning had been a chance meeting, she reminded herself. If she hadn't happened to go jogging, would she ever have seen him again?

"I was planning to take Jessie to the children's museum in Indianapolis next weekend."

"What did you do for excuses before you had Jessie?"

"That's not fair."

In the street, a car door slammed. He swore under his breath.

"You don't want me," Meg argued. "I'm just the first new woman after your divorce."

"Actually, you're not."

She flinched. "Okay. That's all the more reason to call this off. Look, for the hundredth time, I don't fit in your world. You don't fit in mine. It's better that we remain strangers."

"You've got the kind of style that fits in anybody's world. Besides, we're already past being strangers." A pulse ticked in his temple. "But I don't like teases. In fact, a divorcée who's a tease is a contradiction in terms."

She slapped him, hard.

He smiled thinly, distorting the red hand print on his cheek. "Congratulations."

"For what?"

"You've just played too hard to get."

"Good!"

"Good-bye, you mean." He strode to the door, flung it open, and stomped out. The door hit the wall, rattling the Van Gogh print.

Meg listened to his footsteps echoing up the stairwell.

She rushed to the window. "I'm sorry, I'm sorry," she whispered to herself. "Oh, Cash, I'm such a fool."

He left the building and flung himself into the waiting Continental before she could call out. He didn't look up. The car screeched away. Brenda Garrison was driving.

Numbly, Meg went to clean up the kitchen. It looked as if a tornado had made breakfast in it.

CHAPTER FOUR

TWO MORNINGS LATER, as Meg and Jessie were leaving the apartment, a delivery boy arrived with a showy pot of spider mums.

Jessie jumped up and down, clapping her hands. "Oh! They're so pretty! Who are they from?"

"There's no card." Meg carried them to the coffee table. "It's not my birthday or anything." David crossed her mind. No, not him. Not after the kind of divorce they'd had. "It must be a mistake." She checked her watch. "You're going to be late for camp. I'll call the florist when I get back."

But errands kept her downtown until day camp let out. When she and Jessie returned to the apartment late that afternoon, Ruth was waiting in the opposite doorway.

"There you are! I'm about dead with curiosity!" She waved them into her living room. "I've been accepting deliveries for you all day. Just look."

"Roses!" Jessie shouted.

"And gladioli." Ruth said.

"And daisies," Meg murmured.

"Are they all for us?" Jessie cried. "Where'll we put them?"

Meg picked up an arrangement of carnations, baby's breath, and fern. She turned it around, studying its angles. "We could take some to the hospital and some to the nursing home. That is, if this isn't all a big mistake." But somehow she knew it wasn't.

"There's a card in the orchids," Ruth prodded.

"Orchids?" She lifted them from an end table. They were almost too beautiful.

Meg, the card read, *before you cart all of these off to your favorite charity, please decide on something to keep for yourself. Cash.*

"Meg? Meg!" Jessie tugged at her sleeve. "Why are you crying?"

"I'm not crying."

"Are too! I see a tear!"

"There." Meg wiped at her cheek. "Come on, goofball, and help me carry these across the hall."

She found the number of Cash's Washington office on a handout from her citizens' action group. She gave the answering voice her name and the message, "Thanks."

The voice repeated Meg's name carefully. "Hold one moment, please."

"No, I don't—hello? Hello?"

"Meg!" Cash's vitality sizzled across the miles.

"Oh, I didn't ask to speak to you. I mean, I don't want to disturb—"

"I told my secretary to put your call through whenever it came. Glad I was in my office."

"How did you know I'd call? I might have written a letter."

"Not you. You're the straightforward type," he said.

"I didn't realize I came across like Clint Eastwood."

"Now, would I send him flowers?" Cash chuckled.

"I'm surprised to hear from you at all."

"I decided that a nice lady like you deserves another chance with a terrific guy like me."

She laughed. "You're impossible."

"For you, I'm not only possible, I'm easy."

Heat fanned up the neck of her blouse. Her mind went on hold.

"Which ones did you decide to keep?" he asked.

The heat hit her cheeks. "The Norfolk pine, because it will last. And the orchids. No woman alive could resist orchids. Oh, and Jessie would like the violets in her room. Thank you. More than I can say." She swallowed the lump in her throat. "I don't know whether your note was to tease me or not, but I'm glad I can make so many people happy with your gift. It means a lot to me to be able to do that." How could you know me so well? she wondered.

"There's something you can do for me," he said.

"Name it."

"Let me send you a plane ticket to Washington."

"Not that."

"Maybe you don't understand what I'm asking. I want you to come during the week. Most weekends are out anyway, because I'll be home campaigning. It'll be hectic, and we might not even see that much of each other. But I want you to get a firsthand taste of the life I lead here."

"Why?"

"To help you understand me."

Why? she didn't ask.

"The other reason is obvious. I want to see you. Middle of next week? We'll fly back to Masefield together on the weekend. I have several appearances to make there."

"Well. I . . . I appreciate the invitation. Could you hold on a minute?" Meg laid down the receiver. She leaned her back against the wall and closed her eyes. She smelled the flowers in the living room, heard *Sesame Street* going on the television, tasted cold metal. It was the taste of fear. All at once she wanted a cup of strong black tea. She filled the teakettle and set it on a burner. The flame was an unusually deep blue. She picked up the phone again. "On one condition: I buy my own ticket."

He laughed. "Have it your way. Come by covered wagon if you want to. I'll be counting the hours."

Seven days later, as her plane made its approach to Washington National Airport, Meg remembered his words with a twinge. She hadn't spoken to Cash again. Apparently, he had turned the counting of the hours over to his secretary.

The pilot was alerting his passengers to a bird's-eye view of the nation's capital. She looked out into a brilliantly clear day. In a few minutes she would be flinging herself into Cash's arms, and everything would be all right. She looked down, pulse racing.

The flight pattern followed the Potomac River. Ahead on the left, she glimpsed the Washington Monument and the Capitol dome, sparkling in the sun. She consulted the map spread on her knees. Yes, there on the other end of the reflecting pool was the Lincoln Memorial. And there the Mall! The White House! and there by the Tidal Basin, the Jefferson Memorial . . . and Cash was part of it all. He was part of the process that made it all mean something.

On the ground, her anticipation blurred everything. She looked for Cash out the windows of the plane as she stood in line in the aisle. She expected to see him hurrying toward her as she stepped off the plane, as she left the waiting room, and finally in the interminable hallways, as she was sucked along in a stream of passengers bound for the baggage claim area. She strained to hear her name over the public address system. Any minute now, any second...

Waiting for her suitcase to appear on the carousel, she kept searching doors, windows, faces. Her suitcase appeared. Had she arrived on the wrong day? Had her messages never reached him? She got out her ticket and read it over. She put it away and started for a bank of phones. A little girl in pigtails skipped by, and she thought of Jessie. She should never have left Jessie in those circumstances. Maybe she should call home first...

"Meg? I'm Brenda Garrison. Cash asked me to meet you." Her handshake, like her suit, was strictly business.

"Hello." Meg tried to match Brenda's crisp cordiality. "Where's Cash?"

"The House is still in session. Surely you didn't expect him here."

"Oh no. No. Not at all." Meg coughed. "Well. Thanks for collecting me."

"No problem. The car's this way."

They traded remarks about travel and the weather. Brenda struck Meg as basically likable. Without Cash's tall shadow walking between them, they might have been friends.

During the drive, Brenda pointed out sights.

"How did you start working for Cash?" Meg broke in.

"I've known him since I was a child. Our families knew each other. In fact, he started out in my father's law firm." Brenda laughed and reddened, which made her look even younger. "Would you believe that when I was in high school, before my first formal dance, Cash taught me to waltz in our living room?"

"Really."

"I studied political science in college," Brenda went

on, "because Cash thought—" She sat up straighter and said in her business voice again, "This is an interesting street. We'll go this way."

In the lane next to them, in a chauffered limousine, sat one of the justices of the Supreme Court, a study in gray. Suddenly Meg felt all wrong, as if she had just awakened to find herself on a movie set and was the only one who didn't know her lines. In fact, she wasn't even sure what character she was playing. She felt that way until she and Brenda parked and were actually walking down a hall in the Rayburn Building. Then excitement took over. She passed a famous face, smelled coffee, heard bright chatter and the clatter of office machines. The air hummed with purpose and power, or maybe just with the twanging of her nerves.

"Here we are." Brenda showed her past a door with Cash's name on it. Meg quailed. Her face was too tight to smile.

It was an outer office. A receptionist smiled from a desk on the left. Around a desk on the right stood two women and a man, examining a letter. Meg took in their impeccable clothes. Finding a good dry cleaner must rank right up there with reducing the national debt, she thought.

The receptionist gave her a friendly, assessing smile. "He isn't in. Would you like some coffee? No? Then just have a seat."

"I'll be getting back to work," Brenda said. She was very pale. Without staying for Meg's thanks, she shut herself in an office behind the reception area.

Meg sat down next to a couple with two half-grown boys, probably a farm family from Masefield County on their summer vacation. Staffers came and went out of a big office to the right. Cash's office was to the left of the reception area. Meg smoothed the skirt of her sprigged challis dress and crossed her feet at the ankles, wondering why she had ever imagined that a peasant dress and funky straw sandals were the proper attire for visiting a congressman. The world's oldest flower child, she thought, and starting to wilt around the edges.

The minutes ticked by.

The farm family shuffled to their feet. Cash stood in the outer doorway, glowing with the sight of her. Of *her*. Smiling, she sent herself to him through her eyes. She had a split-second sensation that without moving they were rushing toward each other, colliding joyously.

"Glad you could keep our appointment, Ms. Birdsong," he said, poker-faced. "If you'd care to step into my office, I'll be with you shortly."

"Thank you, sir." Solemnly she crossed to the indicated door. The receptionist had pulled such a straight face that she looked like a horse crunching a lump of sugar.

His office was furnished with enough style to impress, but without the expense that might make a citizen wonder where his tax dollars were going. One wall held photographs of Cash with various citizens' groups and political luminaries, including one with the president. Meg had memorized all the faces and was considering counting the buttons on the men's suits when the door behind her opened and shut.

She wheeled. Cash crushed her to him. They kissed, then stood clinging to each other for a long time.

"I remember that: the way your hair smells," he murmured. "Makes me think of one of those meadows Renoir painted. Warm and sweet." He pushed her out from him a little and looked her up and down. After that they stood grinning, arms loosely around each other's waists. "Sorry I couldn't meet the plane."

"Yes, I kept expecting the crowds to part like the Red Sea and there you would be. Is this a typical day?"

"Not anymore." He pulled her against him, and his lips fell on hers with the hot, velvet caress of the sun and fruits and grasses of those Renoir meadows.

Later, as she rested her cheek against his shoulder

and he stroked her hair, she sensed a restless tension in him.

"There's good news and bad news?" she guessed.

He grunted. "The good news is that you're here."

"And?"

"And I have to go back and vote on a bill. I slipped out during the debate."

"I could go with you. Isn't there a visitors' gallery?"

"Won't work. I have to drop in on a meeting after that. It just came up."

"Does it mean votes?"

"Yes, on a bill I'm cosponsoring."

She smoothed the lapels of his navy pin-stripe suit. Maybe charisma was the ability not to attract lint. That and a full head of hair. She had a theory that given two equally qualified candidates, the one with the most hair would win. Gently, she ruffled the waves at his temples and uncovered threads of silver. He was watching her with concern.

"It's all right." She sighed. "After all, you warned me. Lesson number one in how my elected official spends his time."

"I'll cut it as short as I can."

"Anyway, I've already seen you for five minutes more than I would have if I'd stayed home." She tilted smiling lips to meet his. They kissed slowly, almost thoughtfully. "Where can I wait for you?"

"At my place. You'll be comfortable there."

"Not at a hotel?"

"Surely you didn't come all the way to Washington to spend the night by yourself. You can do that at home."

"Good point." They both laughed. Then Meg said soberly, "Just don't ask Brenda to drive me there. It would be a great embarrassment to both of us."

He rubbed his jaw. "I hadn't thought of that. If you feel uncomfortable—"

"It's not just me. Heavens, Cash, you must realize she's in love with you."

"She's just a kid."

"How old is she?"

He frowned to cover up real surprise.

Men! she thought.

A bell rang.

"That's the signal. I've got to get back." He fished keys out of a pocket. "Look, this one's to the apartment." He scribbled a line on a desk pad. "Here's the address." He strode to the outer office. "Edith," he addressed the receptionist, "could you call a cab?" He turned back to Meg. "Your luggage still in the car? I'll bring it when I come." With a wink, he was gone.

A short time later Meg let herself into a comfortable apartment in Georgetown. Heavy gray drapes and thick blue-gray carpeting cocooned the living room in a reverent hush. She stood a moment, absorbing the vaguely forbidding atmosphere of wealth and breeding, then purposefully turned on a lamp and opened the drapes. "Make yourself at home," she said, just to fracture the quietness. And suddenly she thought of Jessie. Jessie, spending the night on that filthy couch... She crossed to a doorway, saw a phone on a desk, hesitated. Phoning Jessie now would only make her worry more about the child; and there was really nothing to worry about. Of some nameless, faceless permission granter, Meg silently begged, *Just let me have this one time for myself. One night away from other people's problems...*

She wandered aimlessly through the rooms, listening for Cash. Gradually she became aware of a certain schizophrenia in the furnishings. Antique chairs that would have collapsed under his weight mingled grudgingly with heavier, more masculine pieces. The debris of two lives that had never quite joined, she reflected. Why hadn't Marcia taken her half with her? She had kept the Victorian mansion in Cash's district.

Meg strolled into the kitchen. The refrigerator contained a bottle of mineral water, a wedge of Brie, half a lemon, and a can of tennis balls. She glanced a second time into the bedroom, at a bed as big as a football field, and returned to her starting point. From a bookcase she selected a volume of Mencken's essays. She kicked off her shoes and curled up on the couch with it.

The next thing she knew, someone was lifting the book from her hands and kissing her cheek. She sat up into Cash's arms. The windows over his shoulder were black.

"You're so nice to come home to," he murmured, his eyes very dark.

"I can't believe I fell asleep."

He tucked a strand of hair behind her ear. "I'm sorry to be so late. But I have every intention of making it up to you now. Look what the caterer dragged in." A large wicker hamper with a blue satin bow on the handle stood on the coffee table. "We've got pâté, a cold chicken, Asti Spumante, petits fours, the works. We'll eat in, maybe later take a drive along the Potomac. The monuments at night are spectacular. Tomorrow you can see the House at work. There's even a debate on public aid that you might be interested in."

"Will there be time for me to see the National Gallery?"

"By yourself, while I'm answering mail. And tomorrow night there's a dinner party. I'd like you to meet a couple of people. We'll have to catch the earliest flight to Chicago the next morning. It'll be a busy day."

She smoothed the lines in his forehead with a finger. "You *do* work hard."

"You bet." He unbuttoned his vest, stripped off his tie. He slumped forward, elbows on knees, and rubbed his eyes.

She wanted to love away his fatigue, but she kept her

voice tart. "Why, maybe I'll vote for you after all."

"Out of pity?"

"You're about as pitiful as an aircraft carrier."

They ate on a balcony just big enough for a glass-topped table and two wrought iron chairs, overlooking the back of a street of neat brick row houses.

Cash lit a patio candle on the table. "How's Jessie?"

"Jessie's fine, but I'm a little worried about the situation I left her in. If you don't mind, I'd like to give her a quick call after dinner."

"You've never really explained her situation."

"Well, her mother was fourteen when Jessie was born. Unmarried, of course. She had another child, Timmy, a couple of years later, by someone else. Karen isn't a bad woman; she was just too immature to have children. She couldn't support them or take care of them. Jessie told me that once they lived on instant pudding for four days." Meg divided a marinated artichoke heart. "So Karen's children were taken away from her. When she demonstrates that she can hold a job and pay the rent for a certain amount of time, she gets them back. She's doing well and can have Jessie and Timmy for longer and longer visits. But... I just don't know."

"What's bothering you?"

"A feeling. Not any one thing. When I took Jessie's suitcase over today, the apartment was a disaster. Karen's face was bruised. She said she twisted her ankle stepping off a curb, and fell. Somehow I doubt it. And... I don't know, I had a feeling that she was hiding something, some secret."

"Do you think Jessie's in danger?"

"Oh, not from Karen. She loves her kids. However, she's capable of neglecting her responsibilities. She's still only twenty-one, and she likes to have a good time. I guess the truth is, she's years older than twenty-one in experience, but years younger emotionally."

"Call."

"I will. Thanks for understanding."

"You're welcome. But, my dear, there are some things I don't understand."

"Such as?"

"Jonathan."

"Oh. Well, he's a good friend."

"Describe your relationship."

"It's just what I said—friendly."

"How friendly?"

"The old-fashioned kind of friendliness. There's even an old-fashioned term for it. We're keeping company."

"Are you sleeping with him?"

"Cash!"

"Your indignation is charming—if it means no."

"It means that it's none of your business."

"It is if you're going to sleep with me."

"My, aren't we candid."

"It's a candid subject."

She put down her knife and fork. "Can't you imagine a relationship between a man and a woman that doesn't include sex?"

His grin widened. "Not if the woman is you."

"Here, get your mind back on this delicious dinner." She stuffed an olive into his mouth.

As her fingertips touched his lips, he grabbed her wrist. Catching the tip of her index finger lightly between his teeth, he kissed it lingeringly, then sat back, holding her hand in his. "What kind of man would let you fly off to visit another man like this?"

"A good man. A fair man."

"Then I'm neither." He released her hand, looking pleased with himself.

"It's a platonic relationship. That's all," she said.

They finished the meal in a silence that drew them closer.

Cash held his glass over the candle and swirled the

Asti Spumante. They both watched the bubbles sparkle and break on the fire-lit surface. He drained the glass, eyeing her, tigerlike, over the rim.

Meg lifted her face to the breeze. A pock-marked, pewter moon watched her do it. "What about you?" she asked.

"There's no one else."

The wind pulled an iron screen of clouds across the moon. Softly, she said, "I'm so happy right now." She drank quickly, and hissing fire raced into her veins. Maybe too happy, she thought.

He blew out the candle. "I need to check my answering service."

"This late?"

"Yes." Coming around the table, she swayed into him. He steadied her with a hand on her hip. "You didn't have that much to drink, did you?"

"No." She put her arms around his waist, hooking a thumb through a back belt loop. "It's you. Just being with you makes me dizzy."

His lips covered hers, and his hands slid down over her buttocks, easing her against him. She sighed as his tongue entered her mouth. Clasping her hands at the small of his back, she thought that there was nothing he could ask for that she would not give him. Their tongues met, and she stretched, catlike, up against him, coaxing his arousal with nudges of her hips.

"Whoa." He pulled her inside the house. "We have phone calls to make. Remember?"

"I don't even remember my name." Laughing, arms around each other, they stumbled across the living room. "Five minutes," she warned him, as he went into his office/guest room.

"Four."

In the master bedroom, Meg snapped on a bedside lamp, found her address book, and put it by the telephone on the nightstand. She paced the length of the room, quelling the flutters. Then she remembered his touch. In the dresser mirror, she saw that her face showed fear, but there was a mischievous glint in her eyes. She was idly twirling the beaded tassel on the drawstring neckline of her dress when Cash, in shirtsleeves, came up behind her. Strangely detached, she watched him push the dress off her shoulders.

"What's this?" He fingered the lavender satin straps he had uncovered. "I could have sworn you weren't wearing anything under that dress."

"Is that all you've been thinking of?"

"No. I was also thinking of that tattoo." He uncovered it and warmed it with his breath. "I don't run across many tattoos." He kissed it, and her nipples burned.

"Something to remember me by. Old what's-her-name, the one with the tattoo."

He turned her around and stripped down the dress. "I think I'll remember—good Lord."

The top third of her new lavender teddy was see-through lace, as was the bottom third. He wasn't going to get around to noticing the opaque satin middle any time soon.

"Surprise," she said, and was suddenly very much at ease.

"I thought you played hard to get."

"I am hard to get. But easy to keep."

He held out his arms, and she came to him, melting under his exploring hands. With her eyes closed and her palms stroking the rippling muscles of his back, she thought how different she was with Cash from the Meg everyone else knew. Only she herself recognized this boldly sensuous woman. It was the woman she had been years ago, before a failed marriage and a plodding career had ground her down. But, after all, wasn't this why people fell in love? To find the secret, exciting selves they believed existed underneath their everyday personalities?

His hands caressed her hips in hot, seductive circles as he kissed her lips, her throat, her shoulders. Her left shoulder strap fell, and they both looked at how the scalloped lace over her left breast hung only by the stiff nipple. Cash gently squeezed her breast into a harder roundness so that the aureole and nipple swelled free of the lace. His head dipped, and his tongue flicked over the sensitive pinkness.

She moaned, lifted on a tide of ecstasy, her fingers twining in his hair as his tongue probed her cleavage. Then he uncovered her other breast, and the moist warmth of his lips gathered in the tip, his teeth tugging at the nipple.

Suddenly, she was lifted off the floor. "What—?"

"Your blasted phone call. I'm trying to be fair. Better make it now, because you're not going to have another chance all night." He carried her to the bed and playfully dumped her on it. "Twenty-five words or less, okay?" He sprawled down beside her, kicking off his shoes.

Meg kissed his forehead. "This is hurting me as much as it's hurting you." She sat up cross-legged and pulled up her straps. She had just found Karen's number when, behind her, Cash started taking out her hairpins. She giggled.

"I want to see you with your hair down."

She dialed. Her hair cascaded down her back.

Cash combed it out with his fingers. "You're beautiful." He ran a finger down her spine.

"Cut it out."

"Really?"

"No." She smiled over her shoulder. "Have your way with me."

"Ah." He pushed her over, so that she fell on her

side. He stretched out behind her, fitting his body to hers.

"Oh God, Cash, stop it. I can't hold a conversation with you doing that."

"Doing what?" He laid an arm over her, pulling himself closer.

"I can't think. The way you're lying, I can feel...uh, everything."

"Turn over and feel some more."

"Be serious a second. Karen isn't answering."

"Good. Hang up." His hand, warm and heavy, spanned her stomach.

"But she has to be home."

"Says who?" He fondled her breasts. "Hang up. You've done your duty."

"You don't understand. She—oh—" His fingers had crawled inside the lace. "She—she never goes anywhere when the kids are there. She doesn't have a car. And...and there's nowhere to go."

"Frankly, my dear, I don't give a damn. How do I get you out of this thing?"

She pushed his hands away gently but firmly. "I've got a funny feeling about this. Please, love, just a minute longer. I'm going to call Sandy Franklin. She's the caseworker."

He fell heavily on his back and closed his eyes.

Meg leaned over him. "Clown." She gave him a long kiss.

"Foreplay with a telephone. I learn something new every day." He struggled against a grin. "Is this supposed to build my character?"

"You're already a character." She stretched out again, her back to him, and dialed.

Cash stroked the curve of her hip and on down her thigh. Resting his chin on her shoulder, he curled around her. One hand played along the lace edge of her teddy, where it had ridden up high on her hip. As she counted ten rings, his fingers inched teasingly along the line where her tan stopped, moving around to the front.

She shifted slightly away from him. "Sandy doesn't answer either."

"So maybe you aren't the only person out having a good time. Come here." He whipped the receiver out of her hand, got rid of it, and pulled her on top of him.

For a time she was aware only of his sinewy length and hardness, of his kisses, of the roughness of his chest hair where he had unbuttoned his shirt.

"Cash, please!"

"Please, what? Anything you want."

"Please, I have to find out what's going on with Jessie. Something's wrong. I can feel it."

"Later."

"Now. You already agreed."

"Now?" As he pulled her face down for a kiss, his pelvis pushed up. Instinctively, she stiffened to return the enflaming pressure. Then with an exclamation, she rolled away and reached for the phone.

"I'm beginning to lose my sense of humor," he told the ceiling.

"One more call. I swear, if this one doesn't pan out, I'll quit."

Cash asked the ceiling, "Why do I have to be turned on by a decent, responsible woman? Where have all the airheads gone?"

The ringing on the other end of the line broke off. Meg tensed. "Jonathan?"

"Jonathan!" Cash roared.

Meg waved for silence.

"Meg. Hi. How are things?" Jonathan sounded as polite and nonjudgmental as ever.

"I'm fine. The reason I'm calling is that I can't reach Karen or Sandy. Is everything all right there?"

Jonathan cleared his throat. She imagined his long, nervous fingers adjusting his steel-rimmed glasses, imagined the squint in his kindly eyes. "You got my message, I take it."

"No."

"You're"—she felt him steeling himself to say it—"at Delaney's house?"

"Yes."

"I left a message on his answering machine, asking you to call me."

"Hold on a second." Meg muffled the receiver in a pillow and turned on Cash. "Didn't you just check your phone messages?"

"Yep." He laced his fingers behind his head and studied the overhead light fixture. "There was one for you."

"Why didn't you tell me?"

"I was going to, later. I had other things on my mind. I still do."

"Oh, you!" She picked up the phone. "Your message got sidetracked. What is it? Is Jessie okay?"

She listened, asking a question now and then. Her stomach churned. She hung up and bent double, hugging herself. Her body was a cold, silly thing. Slowly, she turned to look at Cash, but he wasn't there. Then she saw him sitting in an armchair at the far end of the room. He had rebuttoned his shirt. His arms lay regally still on the arms of the chair.

"Tell me," he said.

"Karen—Jessie's mother—had a miscarriage this afternoon. Nobody was there but Jessie and little Timmy. Apparently, there was a lot of blood, and Jessie was badly frightened." Meg took a deep breath. "Karen went to pieces—she always does—and the responsibility fell on Jessie. Can you imagine a seven-year-old having to deal with that? And bless her heart, she tried. She ran out and hailed a cab. But"—she began to sob—"the driver wouldn't take them. Didn't want to get involved with an injured party. By the time a neighbor took over, Jessie was hysterical. She didn't understand, of course, and she thought Karen was dying and"—Meg gulped for breath—"I'm sure it all linked up in her mind with something else that happened a long time ago. She saw a shooting, one of her uncles. Do you realize what this trauma could do to her?" She hit her knee with a fist. "I should have been there."

"Nobody can be on call twenty-four hours a day."

She slid off the bed and looked around the room.

"Where's Jessie now?" he asked.

Meg found a tissue and mopped her face. "Asleep. Sandy's got her settled with the foster family that has Timmy. But that's temporary. They don't have room."

"How about the man?"

"He's with Karen. He's been in her life for quite a while, but of course he isn't legally able to take the kids in her absence."

"Your dress is over by the bureau."

"Thanks." She found it and pulled it over her head. From inside it, she said tearfully, "She was calling for me. She wanted me, and I wasn't there."

"It seems to me that everything's under control. The caseworker is on the job. Your friend Jonathan is standing by. She's with her brother."

"She needs me. She's very precariously balanced emotionally." Meg went back to the bed and searched the covers for her hairpins.

"She's asleep."

"She might wake up."

"It's doubtful. If she's as bad off as you say, they've sedated her."

"That's beside the point. I should be there." She began to braid her hair.

"I'll put you on the first flight tomorrow morning."

She wound the thick plait around her head. "I'm sorry, but I'm returning immediately."

"Maybe there isn't another flight tonight."

"I'll go to the airport and wait until I get one."

"Possibly, you could get to Chicago by three A.M. But there won't be a flight to Masefield until tomorrow morning."

"I drove to Chicago. My car is in the parking lot." She stabbed in hairpins, feeling alone in the room. "Wait a minute." She whirled on him. "Why are you giving me an argument about this? You just told me where my dress was."

"Sure. I knew you were going home as soon as you hung up the phone. But I regret it."

"Are you trying to make me feel guilty?"

"No."

She stood stiffly in the middle of the room, facing him. The shadows were harsh and angular. He continued to sit motionless. They were trapped in some ugly modern painting about alienation, she thought.

"Look, Cash, I'm really sorry about this. Terribly sorry. But I don't see what alternative I have. Try to understand, won't you? The timing for us is wrong. I thought Karen was hiding something. I should have trusted my instincts. I probably shouldn't have come."

"You didn't. That is, you never left home." He raised a hand, let it fall like a lifeless thing. "I see now that asking you here was a mistake."

She walked closer to him. He looked bewildered, maybe even hurt. "You're not angry?" she asked.

"No."

"Then why do I feel as if you're driving me away?"

He shrugged. "I'm not driving you away. The choice is yours."

She blinked back tears. "It's a difficult choice."

"Thank you for that."

"Cash, I don't want to make the choice alone."

"You have to. It's your life."

"Maybe some other time—" Her voice broke.

"Remember how you used to argue that there was no room for you in my life? It's turned out the other way around, hasn't it? No room for me in yours." He crossed to the telephone. When he had ordered the taxi, he said, "Better put your shoes on. It'll be here in five minutes." He went back to his chair.

She followed him. There had to be something else to say. "Surely, surely you don't think we could—or I could—I mean, under these circumstances, making love wouldn't—"

"No, it wouldn't." He looked away and seemed faintly embarrassed that she was still there.

"Isn't there anything I can say that will make this right?" she asked as evenly as she could.

"If it hadn't been Jessie, it would have been something else," he mused, as if to himself. "Somehow I knew..."

Everything went red. "Stop being so in control!" she shouted. "You *are* making me feel guilty, and you know it. Can't you think of anybody but yourself, you selfish, egotistical—"

He surged out of the chair and shook her by the shoulders. He was eerily calm. "Be quiet. You're too upset to know what you're saying. Listen, there's nothing for you to do but to go home. There's nothing for me to do but let you go. There will always be this conflict between us. There's no point in trying to save the situation. So let's end it with a little dignity."

She looked deep into his eyes. He had not been acting. He was not trying to manipulate her. He was doing the best he could. Part of his best was not to let her know what he was really feeling.

"One other thing," he said with the same detachment. "If you think you're going home just for Jessie's sake, you'd better think again."

Shock cancelled out speech. She ran from the room. Her mind stayed a roaring blank until she had put on her shoes. When she went back in the bedroom, Cash was on the phone.

"Yeah, I know, but if I had those statistics tonight—

hold on." He watched her pick up her suitcase as if he had never seen anybody pick up one before.

Meg squared her shoulders. "What did you mean, I'm not going home for Jessie's sake? Who else am I doing it for?"

"I want you to think about something on the plane: no matter what you do, no matter how hard you try, you can't be Jessie's mother. She already has one."

"You think I'm doing this for myself?"

He studied her. She saw him try to pull out the famous smile; but it wouldn't hold. Almost gently, he said, "Bye, baby."

It was too late for gentleness. "Don't patronize me. I'm not your baby."

"If you don't watch it, you're going to end up as nobody's baby," Cash said tiredly. "And nobody's mother. Think about it. Hello, Brenda. You still there?"

She didn't have any more tears. She was still dry-eyed and numb when she drove into Masefield with the dawn.

CHAPTER FIVE

"I HAVEN'T SEEN you at one of these before," the woman said to Meg.

"No, I usually work behind the scenes. I'm the liaison with the parent group." They exchanged names. "What would you like me to do?" Meg asked.

"Carry this." The woman gave her a hand-lettered sign: SUPPORT THE RIGHTS OF THE HANDICAPPED.

They joined the circle of picketers in front of the Travelers Inn Convention Center.

"Aren't you a friend of Jonathan Weiss?" Liz, the woman, asked.

"Yes, I am. He'll be marching with the group in the Fourth of July parade tomorrow, but he had something else to do this afternoon. You know, I'm surprised to see such a big turnout for a single member of the state legislature."

Together they surveyed the crowded parking lot. Meg noticed several button-down types, obviously supporters of State Senator Earl Polansky, who was to speak that evening. There were also a line of people in wheelchairs and a group of parents of the handicapped. Most of the others had the jeans-and-fatigues attire and the look of careworn sincerity typical of human-rights and environmental activists. In the eyes of the older ones, the banked fires of the sixties still burned. Other special-issue people had come out of the woodwork too: Several Save the Prairie members stood ready to present the speaker with a bouquet of wildflowers; a green-haired man wearing overalls and a sandwich board advertised the Vegetarian Coalition; a trio in hard hats protested the construction of a nearby nuclear power plant. Meg waved at a young woman in painters' pants and a black T-shirt, a speech therapist at Ingersoll.

"It's like a carnival," Meg said to Liz. "Won't the main issue get lost?"

"I don't think so. Anyway, the majority is concerned with Polansky's efforts to dilute the laws guaranteeing the rights of the handicapped. The media knows who to focus on. But of course the others are here for the exposure too." She pointed to the cars from three television stations.

The mayor of Masefield and her husband arrived to scattered applause.

"But that's what I don't understand," Meg resumed. "Why all the hoopla? Polansky isn't that important, is he?"

"He's not the only one we're aiming at. Some pretty important people have been showing up with him; and this isn't just a state issue. Look." The surge of the crowd swayed them toward a white Mercedes disgorging passengers. Among them Meg recognized the publisher of the *Masefield Gazette,* who was a formidable though indirect force in downstate politics.

"Here we go!" somebody yelled, and the picket line

broke into two rows, flanking the doors of the building.

State Senator Polansky, a florid-faced man with a silver pompadour, moved genially down the gauntlet of demonstrators, flanked by two men who kept his progress steady. At the door, he fielded a question from a demonstrator. Then he was inside.

Boos and hisses. The crowd expanded and contracted randomly, a beehive that had lost its queen.

"Now what?" Meg asked the man next to her. "Is that it?" A murmur from the crowd cut off his reply.

With heavy grace, a black Lincoln Continental swung into the parking lot. Moments later, the legendary Sam DeWitt, as short and solid as a fireplug, but not as friendly-looking, came stalking through the crowd.

Cash ambled at his side. Of course he hadn't changed in the long two weeks since Meg had seen him. He still radiated fitness, style, and confidence. She hadn't changed either, except for losing seven pounds and more hours of sleep than she had the energy to count. She lowered her sign to shield her face.

She heard Cash's voice as he approached; he was alternating greetings and comments. His public laugh rang out. Meg cringed and stared at the ground. Beneath the edge of her sign, she saw Sam DeWitt's glossy brown shoes pass by. The black shoes behind his passed, stopped, returned. The sign was lifted from her hands.

"Hello, Meg." His eyes and voice were depthless, cool.

She twitched her braids back over her shoulders. "Hello."

He looked at something behind her, then fixed his eyes on her again. "What are you doing here?"

"Getting on with my life."

"At my expense?" He looked past her again.

"All I care about is what's on my sign. I didn't know you were going to be here."

"Sure you didn't." He nodded at her NEVER UNDERESTIMATE THE POWER OF A WOMAN T-shirt. "Still wearing your brains up front, I see."

She clenched her teeth to keep her jaw from trembling. Her skin prickled from the stares of the throng. "I'd like my sign back, please."

He slid an arm around her shoulders and raised the sign high. "I'm with you on this," he shouted. "Let's see a big crowd in Springfield when the vote comes up in the fall."

Amid the chorus of amazed cheers, a Channel Seven news camera started purring. Meg held herself stiffly, trying not to feel Cash's arm. "Maybe charisma is just a sixth sense that tells you how to make the most of every opportunity for publicity," she said. He didn't hear her.

"How's Jessie?" he asked out of the side of his mouth.

"Okay now. How's the campaign?"

"Going much better than you and your friends want it to," he said through his teeth, and returned the sign.

"I have no idea what you're talk—"

But Cash was shouldering his way to the entrance of the center, where Sam DeWitt stood watching with an air of shrewd interest. Together they went inside.

His anger lingered around her like the smell of burning tires. With a vague notion of escaping it, she turned. Directly behind her, a teenaged boy held a poster that clearly had been lettered by the same hand as hers: DELANEY: PUPPET OF CORPORATE INTERESTS.

"Hey," the boy brayed to nobody in particular. "How about Dollar Sign Delaney going soft on the handicapped all of a sudden?"

"He was concerned about human rights before you were born," Meg snapped. "Why do you think he went into politics?"

"For the bucks, right?" He laughed toward a knot of boys straddling dirt bikes. "You a *friend* of his?" he asked with nasty emphasis.

"He isn't the enemy. He's our elected representative." How stuffy. She grimaced.

"Not for much longer!" Waving his sign, he shambled, snickering, to join his buddies. They rode away doing wheelies.

Trembling, Meg knelt and retied both shoes. When she looked up, the crowd had thinned.

Liz stood over her. "You okay?"

"Yes." Meg got to her feet. "And don't tell me that the boy had a right to his opinion. I'd have to agree."

It began to rain.

Liz said, "Polansky has agreed to answer our questions when he comes out, so some of us are hanging around. Want to join us?"

"Sure. Can we go inside?"

"The security people say no. The rain won't last long."

Many people retreated to cars, but the diehards huddled on the island of trees that bisected the parking lot, waving signs whenever anyone entered the convention center. Meg sipped coffee from a Styrofoam cup and crouched against the base of an elm, hugging her knees.

It rained harder.

A bony, severe woman with straight blond hair said to her, "It was really great to hear Delaney support us. Was that your doing?"

"No. Nobody tells him what to do."

"He came with Sam DeWitt," a man noted. He regarded Meg with suspicion.

She rested her forehead on her knees. *Whatever, I love him.* She blinked, listened to her thought over again. It was true, but so what? The rain was now a heavy, windless curtain. The tree dripped on her. The lettering on her sign ran. Around her, people discussed Public Law 94-142, which was important to the special-education programs in schools. She kept her head down, wondering why she could organize everybody's life but her own.

After a long time, a man and a woman came out of the convention center, got into a car, and drove away. Then three men exited.

"It's breaking up. Let's get over there," the blond woman ordered.

Grimly, Meg crossed the parking lot with the others, blinking rain out of her eyes. The double doors burst open, and the crowd spilled out fast. She was halfway to them when Cash emerged, his jacket collar turned up, heading straight for her. With a nod, he cut through the front line of demonstrators. Meg stood her ground, in a puddle.

He stopped in front of her, planted his feet apart, and folded his arms.

She lifted her chin. "I came here to demonstrate for an issue. I didn't know you were going to be here. I didn't know about that sign behind me. Would you please move?"

The rain strewed diamonds in his hair. "You'll catch cold."

"I'm tougher than I look."

"But not half as tough as you think you are." He took her arm. "Let's go."

She pulled back. "What the hell do you think you're doing?"

He picked her up by the waist and stuffed her under one arm, so that her head hung down near his knees and her feet kicked out behind.

"I'm infringing on your right to free speech and your right to assembly," he said as he walked. "If you don't like it, that's too bad. I'm bigger than you are."

She couldn't struggle because she couldn't breathe. In front of the upside down convention center, an upside down crowd pointed after them. State Senator Polansky's upside down pompadour gleamed against a black umbrella. A man carrying a news camera ran toward them, like a fly scurrying across a ceiling. Then she was swung upright and dumped in the front seat of the Continental. Cash went around to the driver's side and climbed in.

"Is Mr. DeWitt coming with us?" She put ice in her voice.

"Mr. DeWitt is a man of infinite resources. He can get home on his own." He turned on the ignition.

"I'm dripping on your seat covers."

"They'll survive." He threw the car into reverse, but kept his foot on the brake and glowered at her. "You really didn't know about that sign?"

"Of course not. Anyway, I'm surprised you're so thin-skinned."

"Ordinarily, I'm not." They wheeled away from the newsmen. "But ordinarily, you aren't involved." His eyes flicked to the rearview mirror.

Meg looked back at the crowd gawking after the Continental. "I hope my abduction hasn't hurt your credibility with anybody."

"Or yours. Your friends probably think you're a spy for the corporate puppet now."

"Why did you do it?" she asked.

"Would you have come with me if I'd asked you to?"

She studied the backs of her hands.

He snorted. "I rest my case."

An early dusk was falling with the rain. The streetlights had kicked on. Under them, the pavement glistened like a juicy whip of licorice. The dream machine purred through the Old Town district, an economically fragile area of nostalgia clothing boutiques, new wave hair salons, music stores, and tired bakeries with six-loaf inventories. When they turned down Princeton Street, Meg caught Cash's eye.

"I assumed you were taking me home."

"I am." He flashed the old, easy grin. "My home."

His town house was a narrow, weathered brick building with a lookalike leaning on either shoulder. The one on the left had two broken windows in the second story. Three doors down stood a mom-and-pop grocery store with crates of bananas sitting out front under a green canvas awning. On the next corner, BURGER BAR burned in chubby blue neon. Across the street were yellow brick apartment buildings.

As he unlocked his door, Cash said, "I've come to like it here. It's real. What is it Kerouac says in *The Dharma Bums* about the lunch carts of the world calling to him when he's up on the mountaintop?"

"You read Kerouac? Next you'll be telling me you were in the protest marches."

"I was. As a member of the National Guard."

The darkened vestibule smelled of lemon oil and cedar. Meg sneezed. Water oozed from her beat-up Nikes.

He shook his head. "Come on. You need a hot shower."

She followed him upstairs. "You brought me here to take a shower? I can do that at home."

"You could. But would you? You didn't have enough sense to get in out of the rain."

In the upstairs hall, he handed her a towel from the linen closet. "Give me your clothes. I'll throw them in the dryer."

"Do you realize you're treating me like a child?"

"I never saw anyone who needed it more." He opened the door to the bathroom. "In you go."

"But—" She sneezed messily. Her teeth chattered.

Cash raised an eyebrow.

"Oh, all right." When she handed her clothes out, she asked, "And then what?"

"We can talk. Here's a robe."

She stood under the hot spray until she thought her bones would melt. When she got out of the shower, the bathroom was white with steam. Somewhere, Tschaikovsky was playing. Footsteps crossed beneath her. A teakettle whistled. What had happened to Cash's breakneck schedule? Here in his house, the world dozed in a warm, hidden hollow between afternoon and night. Drying herself, she felt as if she had always lived in this sturdy old structure. Then she recognized the feeling for what it was: the sense of belonging that she often felt in his presence, until one of them shattered it with a sharp remark.

The robe was a chocolate velour kimono piped in cream, with a hood. Before putting it on, she dusted herself with some plain talcum and brushed out her hair, which the plaiting had crinkled. Then she slowly descended the stairs, the robe trailing the ground.

Cash sat in a brown leather armchair in the living room, reading from a folder by the light of a gooseneck lamp. "Have a seat." From the table at his elbow, he handed her a steaming mug. Then he unplugged the telephone.

She took the stool at his feet. "Why do I feel as if I've been called into the principal's office?"

"I don't know." His lips twitched, maybe with amusement and maybe not. "Have you misbehaved?"

The air conditioning was starting her chill all over again. She sipped bouillon and felt better. "Maybe I panicked in Washington. Maybe I didn't handle the situation correctly. Maybe I was unfair to you. But I was still right to come back to Masefield when I did."

"Was I wrong to want you to stay?"

"No, I guess not, not from your point of view."

"So what have we learned from all this?" He was ironic, principallike.

"What we've known from the beginning: that we have different priorities and that our lifestyles don't mesh." *But I love you. I love you.* She couldn't say it. The mug burned her palms.

The music curled around the room. Rain coursed down the bay window to her right.

Finally, she said, "I've been reading some interesting articles about you."

He didn't help her out with so much as a raised eyebrow.

"Porter, in the *Trib*, notices that while you're still a fiscal conservative, your voting has slowly gotten a bit more liberal on social issues."

"It's a matter of public record."

"I know that, but I guess I had to have it pointed out to me." *Why are you being so cold?* she wanted to scream. "Also, there have been hints in the *Gazette* that you're distancing yourself, slowly but surely, from the DeWitt interests. That you feel strong enough to be your own man."

"I have always been my own man." He said it quick and hard, a man swatting a fly.

"I know you have. I didn't mean it that way."

"You damn do-gooders don't know the first thing about surviving in politics. Do you expect me to finance all those TV spots through cute little drives to sell aluminum cans to some recycling center, which will then donate three cents out of every dollar to my campaign chest? *Of course* I have had to deal with people who have real money. And by the way, a lot of those people are sincerely interested in electing the best man. That doesn't mean I've sold my soul."

"But you *are* changing."

"Don't get your hopes up."

She set down the mug and hitched the footstool closer. "Why are you being so difficult? Can't you see I'm trying to apologize? I always thought you were completely rigid in your political beliefs, that you'd be saying the same things in your tenth term that you said in your first. But maybe I was wrong. You're listening, thinking, developing. Even if we never share the same views, I respect that."

"And then there are some of us who are too smug to change."

"If that's the way you feel about me, what am I doing here?"

"Waiting for your clothes to dry."

"That's all?"

They stared at each other. It was a standoff.

"When you walked out on me in Washington," he said slowly, "I forgot you. It was surprisingly easy. But today when I saw you out there, as cute and as nutty as ever, I realized I hadn't forgotten you at all." The glacier in his face broke apart. He held out his arms.

She clambered into his lap and flung her arms around his neck. "The hell with politics. I've missed you."

"I've missed you, too. Even missed how angry you make me sometimes." He stroked her back. She curled up, her cheek against his chest, hearing his heart. She didn't try to keep the robe closed. The room grew dark and secret. Rachmaninoff washed the walls, rolled like a riptide over the soft carpet. Cars swished by beneath the bay window, spraying pale light across the ceiling.

A buzzer sounded.

"That's the dryer," he said.

"I don't care." She raised her head and kissed his chin.

Cash lifted her by the waist and set her on an arm of the chair. "Excuse me." He got up and left the room. She heard him go downstairs. In a minute he appeared in the doorway, holding her clothes. "There wasn't a bra."

"Surely you already knew that from my wet T-shirt." She dangled a bare leg over the chair arm.

"Hard to tell. There's some pretty deceptive lingerie walking around these days."

He looked too innocent. Meg slid off the chair and slunk toward him. She did fine except for tripping on the robe twice. "Can we forget my clothes for a while?"

He raised a palm. She could practically see the cartoon

light bulb go on over his head. "Hold it right there. I left your belt upstairs. I'll get it."

"Cash!" Halfway up the stairs, she caught his arm.

He turned, eyebrows quizzical. "Yes?"

"Do you know what you remind me of? One of those old movies where the hero, a handsome but bumbling professor, keeps not noticing that he's locked in a room with a"— she let the robe slid off one shoulder—"ravishing woman."

Cash scratched his jaw. "You could be right. Darned if you couldn't."

On the landing she caught up with him again, bounced in front of him. "Okay, just tell me the name of the game. I'll play."

"I'll tell you what kind of game we're not playing," he said in a helpful, let's-make-it-simple voice. "We're not playing abbreviated lovemaking. You're too good for me. Gosh, you can think of more ways to get out of making love."

"Now wait a minute."

"No, no, don't try to apologize. I'm just not in your league. I never get too angry to make love, and I never have to make any phone calls at a critical moment. Guess I don't have enough imagination." He went into the bedroom.

Meg hesitated, then followed him.

He was sitting on the bed, threading her belt through the loops of her jeans.

Meg sat down beside him, close.

Cash reached over, pulled the panels of the robe together over her bare thighs, and went back to his task.

She snuggled against him.

"This is getting difficult," he said.

"What is?"

"Getting this belt through. You should get a narrower one."

She knelt on the bed, put her arms around him, and

Into the Whirlwind

whispered in his ear, "I'm not angry now. And Jessie is spending the night with Ruth's little girl."

"So where are you going this evening? Any stray animals out there you have to find a home for?"

"I don't have any plans."

"Oh." Cash worked the belt through the last loop. He folded the jeans and handed them to her. She tossed them over her shoulder.

Gravely, he kissed her, exploring her lips as if he were tasting a subtle new flavor. "I have plans for tonight."

"You do?"

He tilted her chin up. "They were cancelled the minute I saw you."

Meg narrowed her eyes. "Cash Delaney, have you been seducing me by not seducing me?"

He began to laugh, collapsing backward and pulling her with him. They came to rest on their sides, facing each other.

"You big, infuriating—" She started giggling. They nuzzled, kissed.

"You're not so bad at seduction yourself," he murmured, loosening the sash of the robe. "But I'll be happy to take over now."

She sighed contentedly and turned on her back. The robe fell open, and she stretched seductively. "I've always wanted to make love in a big brass bed like this."

He kissed her throat, while he stroked the insides of her thighs with his hands. "It has a certain charm."

She wound her fingers in his hair and raised his head so that she could kiss him on the mouth. "Have you made love to many women in this bed?" When he didn't answer, she pushed with her feet until she had scooted up to the head of the bed and lay propped against the pillows. "Well?"

With a melting grin, he moved up to sit beside her. He finished removing the robe and began to fondle her breasts. "The fact that we both have sexual experience is what makes this so exciting. Don't you agree?"

"You're right." She put her arms around his shoulders, and her breasts shifted forward, filling his hands. "I don't want to think of anyone but you right now." As they kissed, she unbuttoned his shirt. "Thanks for kidnapping me," she mumbled.

"It was that wet T-shirt," he growled, continuing to caress her breasts. "You were a hazard to traffic. It was my civic duty to get you out of the public eye...and into my bed."

"I didn't think it would rain..." She slid her hands inside his shirt and stroked his rock-hard torso.

He stood up and stripped off his clothes. She had seen him naked in her fantasies; now she knew she hadn't done justice to the reality. Tentatively, she reached out to him; he took her hands and guided them. Then he lay down, burying his face in her belly, his tongue circling her navel. With a shudder of pleasure, she curled over him, her knees gripping him, her breasts against his hair.

"I love you, I love you," she whispered over and over, holding him to her.

He didn't answer, but she forgot that in the whirlwind of passion that possessed them, the spiraling intensity of their kisses. His hands and lips, roaming her at will, made her cry out with a complete delight that yet carried with it an insatiable desire for more. In a low, husky voice that she hardly recognized, she heard herself urging him on, begging, cajoling, matching the increasing wildness of his conquest. When at last he stretched out on top of her, the hot pressure of his arousal sent her into a new explosion of sensation. Feverishly, she stroked his back, shoulders, and buttocks as their kisses tore, reached deeper and deeper into brilliantly dark levels of feeling, and his tongue plunged again and again through her unbridled, ecstatic moans. Then his knees spread her legs, and she gripped him hard, her nails raking his back, and she cried out as he thrust inside her. She hung on as she was torn away from herself and joined with him in a surging rhythm, a tremendous, shoreless tide of wild, erotic motion, swirling around the red roaring deep inside her, where he was. Together they rode the headlong current of ecstasy until, in a soaring joyous leap, they fell over the edge of the world...

Sometime later, as she cradled his damp, relaxing body, he drawled in her ear, "No wonder you're smug. Don't ever change. Don't ever change anything about you."

They lay in bed, holding hands, the rain whispering old rumors at the window. After a long time, Meg said, "It's all right if it goes nowhere. I just want to know now."

Cash yawned, sat up. Touching thumb to thumb and index finger to index finger, he made a circle and held it over her head. "Your halo is ready, madam."

She batted the halo away. "Well, somebody has to be noble about this."

"I don't see why. There's no sacrifice involved."

"Maybe not for you." She looked away.

He turned her head back and held it there, his knuckles against her cheek. "Between your commitments and mine, it's going to be hard for us to see much of each other. But I'd like to try. I don't want to be without you for two weeks again." He drew her to him in a body-long embrace. "Do you think a selfish, egotistical bastard and a knee-jerk martyr can find happiness together?"

Against his shoulder, she said, "Yes, I think so. And I promise you won't have to kidnap me the next time you want me. Just whistle."

He whistled.

CHAPTER SIX

THE MASEFIELD CENTRAL High School band finished the "Washington Post March" marking time, did a crisp military turn, and stepped off down Sangamon Boulevard. The unicycle team behind them broke off the figure eights, formed rows, and rolled forward.

"Ready, Brownies?" Meg called. "Monica, leave Cissie alone. Stay in your rows. Jill, you dropped your hat."

"Miz Birdsong, can I have some juice? I'm hot."

"All right, Betsy. Everybody else, one-two, one-two." Meg stepped out of line, gave Betsy a cup of orange juice from the Thermos jug, and hustled back to her place beside Jessie.

"I want to be in the Fourth of July parade every year! Can I?" Jessie exclaimed. "Have you seen my mom yet?"

"No, but I'm sure she'll be here if she can, Jess. Keep looking for her. We have a long way to go yet."

They hit Sangamon and Eighth, where the rowdier university students traditionally gathered. Meg started the children singing the Brownie song "I've Got Something in My Pocket," and the students clapped, whistled, and danced in the gutters.

Meg gave a little skip. It was a silly and wonderful day. High above the parade, a giant hot air balloon disguised as a tomato advertised a local pizzeria. Two punkers on roller skates stroked by, mohawk haircuts slicing the breeze. Behind the Brownies, the seventeen-year-old Miss Fourth of July threw kisses and hard candy from a 1955 Thunderbird. Meg craned to see around the band. Somewhere near the head of the parade, Cash should be riding in a red Cadillac convertible. She grinned ear to ear.

"Why spend our short time together sleeping?" he'd whispered near dawn, and she had laughed out loud, because she was already awake and feeling the same way...

The Brownies were shouting and waving to a Cookie Monster who was handing out balloons along the side. Meg looked back toward where Jonathan would be marching with the citizens' group, but she couldn't see him. A dark arrow pierced the shining hour. They needed to talk. Dear, good Jonathan. No high highs with him, but no low lows either. He would be so much safer.

They passed the university and entered Campustown, marching between stores sporting American flags and red-white-and-blue clearance-sale signs. Firecrackers rattled in side streets. The time and temperature sign on the bank registered ninety-one degrees Fahrenheit. Shoelaces came untied, ponytails drooped, Brownie beanies slid down over ears. The other troop leader dropped out with Megan, who had skinned her knee. Blinking sweat out of her eyes, Meg noticed a commotion along the right side of the parade route. Her heart soared. Cash was glad-handing his way back toward them.

"You look like you could use some help." He grinned,

a subtle declaration of ownership in the way he looked at her.

"Well, I do feel like the old woman who lived in a shoe."

"History doesn't tell us anything about an old man in the shoe, but there must have been one."

"He was probably tall, dark, and hardly ever home."

"A political type, out lobbying for the shoe industry." He waved at two women holding small American flags. "Hi, there. How ya doing?"

Jessie was in front of him, walking backward. "Are you the man that sent the flowers?"

"I am. Did you enjoy them?"

"My violet died." She danced away.

"Miz Birdsong, Cissie stepped on me!"

"Well, she wouldn't get out of the way!"

"Can I have some juice?"

"Can I too? I'm getting a blister."

"Can we ride in a car? Megan got to!"

"The Brownie vote isn't as easy to capture as I thought." Cash chuckled.

"You're getting enough others." The sight of Delaney with the Brownies was as sweet as apple pie to the sentimental crowd. Even people who looked like Saunders supporters were applauding.

"I may march here every year," he said. "Hello there! Hi, how are you?"

"Is your Cadillac empty?" she asked.

"No, there are three lovely Delaney fans riding in it, naturally giving out free fans."

"'Delaney for Congress' printed on one side and the Sermon on the Mount on the other?"

"Are you needling me?" he demanded jovially. "Are you poking fun?"

"Why *did* you become a Brownie, Congressman?"

"To win votes. I mean to win your vote."

"Uh-huh."

"Hello, Mr. Thomas. Good to see you!" He sprinted back to shake hands with a man in a lawn chair.

A thin, pale woman pushed her way to the edge of the crowd, hand raised tentatively.

Meg said, "Jessie, look!"

With a shout, Jessie ran full tilt into the woman's arms.

Meg winced. Then she was all right. Cash returned. "Bless her. I was so afraid she wouldn't show," Meg said.

"Jessie's mother?"

"Yes." Behind Miss Fourth of July, a community chorus on a flatbed truck broke into "Up a Lazy River." "I've been thinking about what you said in Washington; that Jessie already has a mother."

"I was pretty rough on you."

"I needed it. I still do."

He squeezed her hand. "You're going to be all right." Their eyes locked. "I'll see that you are."

"Miz Birdsong, can I walk up front with Sarah?"

"Can we get some balloons?"

He laughed. "I'd better go back. I'm supposed to be on the reviewing stand at Chicago Street before the parade gets there."

"Bye." She blew him a tiny kiss and, weak-kneed, tried not to trip and fall as she watched him lope away. The next time she saw him, he was sitting on the reviewing stand next to the mayor. Straight-faced, he winked. Then she was past him. Only then did it occur to her that they had made no definite plans for seeing each other again.

At home, after she had distributed all the limp Brownies to their families, she poured lemonade for herself and Jessie, put her feet up, and opened the morning paper. A picture of her was on page two, her patched blue-jeaned rear in the air, as an angry Cash carried her to the car. CONGRESSMAN AND DEMONSTRATOR CLASH screamed the headline. The accompanying story was short and bewildering. Cash could not be reached for an explanation, and the head of his district office wasn't talking. But Meg was identified by name, address, and occupation. Moreover, someone on Princeton Street had seen them go into Cash's town house together.

"Lord." She fanned away a hot flash.

Jessie, lying on the floor, looked up from her coloring book. "It's past lunchtime. Can we have hot dogs?"

"Mmmm." The next page listed the local Fourth of July activities. She pondered one item. Why hadn't he told her?

"And barbecued potato chips," Jessie said, smacking her lips. "And can I have an ice cream sandwich too?"

"Mmmm."

"Can I have a dinosaur?"

"Mmmm."

Jessie rolled over, clutching her stomach. "Ha-ha, you're not listening. Ha-ha-ha!"

Meg grinned. "Hey, kid, where'd you get the weird sense of humor?"

"From you! Can I have a fried tarantula? Ooooh, gross!"

"I have a better idea." She tore out the picture and put it in her purse. "We're going out to lunch."

When they drove up to the fairgrounds, the parking lot was nearly full.

"The fair!" Jessie shouted. "Can I go on the Bullet?"

"The fair isn't on now. We're going to a pig roast for Mr. Delaney. It's to raise money for his campaign."

"That's as gross as a fried tarantula."

The fat woman selling tickets raised her eyebrows as Meg counted out twenty-five one-dollar bills.

"My mad money," Meg apologized.

"Children under twelve are free."

"I was hoping you'd say that."

"Aren't there even going to be any animals?" Jessie demanded.

The fat woman said, "There's a roast pig."

They followed the sound of country music to a big orange-and-blue canopy on the midway. The size of the crowd under it, eating at picnic tables or standing in small groups, surprised Meg. Tables of food stretched down one side, culminating in an enormous gas grill loaned by a local rib house and presided over by a man wearing a chef's hat and a KISS THE COOK apron. Across the far end stretched a low stage, where Junior and the Illinois Playboys were belting out "Heart Mender." Near the center of the tent, where the tables were the thickest, stood Cash, surrounded by well-wishers. Meg pulled Jessie to a halt.

He was working the crowd slowly and steadily with Roger, his district head, at his elbow. She soon saw that they made a smooth team. Like a ventriloquist, scarcely moving his lips, Roger fed Cash information about the loyal unknowns waiting to speak with him.

"Are you Eugene Watson?" Cash boomed, pumping a man's hand. "I thought so. You look a lot like your grandfather. I knew him years ago. A fine man."

Eugene Watson reddened, nodded, and suddenly thought much more highly of old Grandpa.

But Cash was genuinely interested in these people, Meg chided herself. He might look like a king and he might sometimes vote like a representative from Mount Olympus, but today he was a democrat, with a small *d*.

"There's Mr. Delaney!" Jessie shouted.

"Yes, I know."

"Can we go talk to him?"

Something held her back. "I thought you were starving."

Moving down the food line, she kept observing Cash

joke, hug, slap backs, and pause for short, intense conversations.

"What's so funny?" Jessie asked her.

"What? Oh, I was just imagining how surprised Mr. Delaney will be when he gets around to us."

"Do they have Cokes? I'm thirsty."

"Maybe down at the end." Meg leaned around the line to see. Halfway to the end, a heavyset man in a baby blue leisure suit stared back at her. He nudged the woman beside him and commented to her out of the corner of his mouth.

Meg drew back. But she had already seen a ripple of information pass on down the line.

"Why are we going back here?" Jessie complained when their plates were full. "I want to sit up near the band."

"It's cooler here." Meg set her plate on an empty table in the last row. She remembered a saying of Jonathan's: *Children make liars of us by being so truthful.* Cash bent over a table of well-dressed couples, punctuating his remarks with chops of his right hand. The band was roaring, "Rock and Roll is King."

All at once, Meg picked up on a conversation to her right.

"—damn picture in the paper this morning. Somebody's got to say something to him about her."

"Not me. I want to live to see my children grow up."

"Maybe Brenda," a third man put in.

"No, she's too involved herself. Damn near died when the woman showed up in D.C."

"She must be some chick. Have you seen her?"

"There was another picture taken with him at Ingersoll School back in June. Roger said he marched part of the way with her in the parade this morning."

"She didn't have anything to do with his divorce, did she?"

"Don't think so. On the other hand, we started noticing her right after Marcia made the announcement."

"This lady could be a real image problem. You know, the divorce didn't hurt him as bad as we thought. A lot of people can identify with a personal problem like that. Besides, he's looking good as a bachelor. The old ladies want to mother him, and the young ones—I don't have to tell you. But *nobody*, male or female, wants to see him make a fool of himself the way he did yesterday over a—"

"Especially if she's the wrong kind, imagewise."

"Yeah. If we could find another Marcia, we'd be in business. Camelot revisited. But this one—even he'd admit she's not the right type for a man in his position."

Someone guffawed. "You fellows are getting paranoid. Let the man have a little fun. This won't last. I knew him before Marcia, and I can guarantee that. Besides, what he does in private is his business."

"But it's getting public."

"There are still more than enough people who vote the issues or straight ticket." Heavy sarcasm.

"As long as she doesn't influence his politics. I heard she's a socialist."

"Now there, boys, is the real problem. He's ahead in the latest poll. But if his ideological base shifts even a quarter of an inch..."

"Okay, she has to go. I'll see what I can do after this is over. Talk to you later." A bench creaked and there was the sound of footsteps.

Sparks danced before Meg's eyes. Her voice came from a long way off. "How's lunch, Jessie?"

"Sort of good and sort of yucky. Why aren't you eating?"

"I will." She blotted her forehead with a napkin. "It's awfully hot in here. Maybe we should—"

At the applause, she looked up. Every table was full. People lined the sides two deep. Cash stood onstage to the right of the band, arms raised triumphantly. His face glistened. His shirt clung limply to his magnificent physique. He exuded raw attractiveness and power. She couldn't believe that only hours before, she had lain in his arms. The ringing noise in her ears must be the aftershock of their worlds wrenching apart again.

Pushing aside the microphone, he began to thank individuals and to speak of the coming victory, made possible by the good friends gathered around him today...

Jessie was combing out the hair of her Golden Dream Barbie and rhythmically kicking the table leg. Meg picked up her purse, tensed to stand, touched Jessie's arm...

The entire audience turned and looked at them.

Her stomach did a fast elevator drop.

The men who had been discussing her stood up.

She breathed again. Cash was singling them out, not her. She clapped weakly.

But Cash's attention, leaving the honorees, fell on her. His features stiffened. He stopped applauding. Quickly, he recovered, picked up his patter. But his brows remained stern.

With a finger to her lips, Meg signaled Jessie to be silent. Then she took her hand and headed for fresh air.

Outside the canopy, she looked back. All eyes were on Cash. Flies floated dopily through the smoke around the grill. DELANEY FOR CONGRESS fans waved lazily to and fro.

Jessie stooped to pick up a DELANEY FOR CONGRESS button from the grass. "Can we go swimming today?"

"Maybe. Come on."

Meg didn't quite know what she was going to do, but she knew she had to do it. On tiptoe, she made her way down the side of the canopy until she was even with the stage. Between onlookers, she glimpsed Cash in profile, heard his voice building to an emotional climax. Damn, he's good, she thought. Plays them like a violin.

She led Jessie around behind the stage.

"What are we—?"

"Quiet. Watch your feet." They picked their way across a maze of electrical cables leading to the band's equipment. The drummer of the Playboys, perched on a crate with a hand-rolled smoke, watched them indifferently. Meg stopped directly behind Cash, several yards back of the stage, where she was hidden from the audience. Three low wooden steps provided a back exit from the stage. Beside them lounged a blond, twentyish man in a safari suit with a camera slung around his neck.

Jessie hopped from one foot to the other. "I'm tired."

"You can sit on those steps."

Brenda Garrison, pale with shock, barred the way. "Meg, what are you doing here? What can you be thinking of?"

"Hi, Brenda. I just wanted to say hello to Cash."

"Don't you realize what an uproar you caused yesterday? Haven't you done enough?"

"It took two of us, may I remind you. But I wanted to say something to him about that before—"

"You don't need to say anything." The whites of Brenda's eyes widened. "Just go. Now. Before there's any trouble."

"I thought this event was open to anyone with the price of a ticket."

Brenda stepped closer. "Let me explain something you should already know. Fundraisers like this are strictly between the candidate and his very loyal supporters and friends. It's part of the internal reward structure of the party, a chance for Cash to thank personally everybody who's fighting in the trenches for him. Do you understand? It's a love feast. It's his show, and it's their show. Don't upstage them."

"I wasn't going to." Meg started moving backward.

Brenda hesitated, then visibly decided to fire the heavy artillery. "Don't you think he'd have asked you to come if he'd wanted you here?"

Meg was brought up short. She hesitated, then said, "I'm sorry, I shouldn't have come. I . . . I see that now."

Brenda sighed and closed her eyes with relief. When she opened them, there was renewed intensity in her expression. "Thank you. Thank you for understanding. You see, he's among friends here. Nobody's going to ask any sticky questions. He can relax and not have to worry about defending himself. I know you wouldn't want to ruin that."

"No."

"Give him a break, Meg. He needs it. Besides, I don't see any convincing way to explain what happened yesterday. We have to hope it blows over soon or people will start questioning his judgment. They'll wonder just how often he goes out of control. Remember what happend in the 'Seventy-two campaign when Muskie cried in public? It was before my time, but the example is still raised. You can be sure that Saunders will capitalize on Cash's behavior yesterday."

"He's fair."

"He wants to win. Be realistic."

"All right, all right. I'll go." Her voice was strangled and lumpy. "Jessie?"

Brenda gasped. "Oh my God."

"And he sent lots of flowers," Jessie was telling the man in the safari suit, who was holding out a small tape recorder. "Every kind of flower you can imagine, even orchids. And Meg cried, but she was happy and —"

A roar of applause drowned her out. Meg dashed at her and grabbed her by the hand. "Come on, honey."

The band started playing "Yankee Doodle."

"Aren't we going to wait for Mr. Delaney?"

"No. Let's go."

"What's going on?" Cash stood on the steps, fists on hips, frowning at them. The noise of the band broke over his back and engulfed their feeble replies.

"Congressman!" the reporter said. "I'd like to get a comment on the incident at the Travelers Inn yesterday. Is this lady here—"

"Meg?" Angry puzzlement contorted his face.

"No! I didn't—I mean, I'm not with him. I just came to—"

The reporter wheeled on her, stuffing the tape recorder in a pocket and raising his camera.

Meg jerked Jessie off her feet and ran.

"Where are we going?" Jessie squealed.

"Home. Swimming. I don't know."

That night at the Masefield University stadium, Jessie howled with delight at the fireworks bursting above them. But Meg kept her eyes on the dignitaries' box on the fifty-yard line. Every time the sky lit up, she had another glimpse of Cash surrounded by the right people, including Brenda. And with each flash of light she wondered if she was seeing him in person for the last time.

CHAPTER SEVEN

THE PHONE. RINGING. Again. Again. Again.

"'Lo."

"Where have you been?"

"Mmmf." Meg rolled over, clutching the pillow. Warm pillow, soft.

"Meg, wake up!"

Cash! She sat up, wide awake, heart thudding. "Cash...do...do you realize what time it is?"

"Late. Do you remember the question?"

"Question. Where I was?" She yawned, a fake. "I took Jessie camping at Turkey Run. Then we went to see my folks in Fort Wayne."

"Why?"

"Why? To have fun, take a vacation."

"And to make yourself scarce? To get away from me?"

"I had to get permission ahead of time to take her out of state. It wasn't a spur of the moment thing. You can check it out."

"Somebody somewhere is doing without any coincidences in his life. You've got a double share."

She sat awhile. "Your campaign doesn't need me."

"But I do."

"Campaign rhetoric?"

"I'm not going to argue over the phone, Meg. Can you spend the afternoon with me?"

She felt a muscle cramp in her shoulder. She rubbed at it. "I don't think that would be a good idea."

She heard a crack, as if he'd snapped a pencil in two. "I'll pick you up in an hour." He hung up.

Fifty minutes later, the big black car double-parked in front of the apartment building. Meg leaned out the window and motioned for Cash to come upstairs. He shook his head. So she wouldn't have a chance to talk him out of it.

Getting in beside him moments later, she said, "In this neighborhood, in this car, you're about an inconspicuous as an Abe Lincoln lookalike with his hair on fire."

Cash leaned over and kissed her on the cheek. He wasn't angry. The essence of him—minty after shave; thick, lowered lashes; shiny hairs in the open neck of his Western-cut shirt; heavy shoulders; chiseled mouth; long legs in tight jeans—swept weakness through her.

"Good morning." He winked and set the car in motion.

"Haven't your advisers talked to you about me?"

"They have. I told them what they could do with their advice, in intricate detail." He beat a light, slowed again. "Did something happen at the fairgrounds that I don't know about?"

"I overheard some talk. It seems I'm quite a liability to you."

"You let me worry about that." He glanced at her. "Whatever possessed you to pay good money to attend that thing?"

"I've asked myself that a thousand times since then."

She shrugged. "I guess the answer is I couldn't stay away. I wanted to see you again, wanted to see what you were like at one of those gatherings. I went on impulse. Then almost as soon as I got there, I realized it was a mistake. I hadn't suspected I wouldn't be welcome. No, don't interrupt. It doesn't matter." She laid a hand on his arm. "I don't want to do anything else to jeopardize your campaign. That's why I didn't want to go anywhere with you today. Isn't it better if we aren't seen together?"

"But if I don't see you often enough, I tend to kidnap you in parking lots." He grinned wryly. "So you're an even bigger liability when you stay away. But about the fundraiser—I really didn't think about inviting you at all. I'm not used to thinking about you in my schedule. I'll do better from now on. Okay?"

"Okay." She felt relieved.

"Also, I didn't expect you to drop out of sight like you did," he continued. "I thought social workers were trained in confrontation."

"I wish there weren't, but there's a big difference between how I behave professionally and how I conduct my personal life," she explained.

"Same with me." He wiggled his eyebrows like Groucho Marx. "Thank goodness."

"Cash, what do you want me to do? I'm confused."

He reached for her hand. "Be there when I need you. But it's probably true that we should avoid publicity, at least until we can behave rationally together."

"Do you suppose that day will ever come?"

"Not in private, I hope."

She laughed against his shoulder. Everything was all right again. But she thought to herself, What about what *I* need?

"There's nothing scandalous about our seeing each other," he resumed. "I just can't afford to look out of control. And then there's the matter of Marcia's popularity. A certain type of voter will choose to see my interest in you as infidelity, despite the divorce. Masefield may be liberal for this district, but it's pretty conservative when compared with other parts of the country." He kissed her knuckles. "Relax. You aren't nearly as controversial as my stand on aid to Central America. This too shall pass."

She played with his hand, running her finger over the blunt-cut nails, stroking the back. At the beginning, she'd fantasized about having him all to herself in private. Now that the deal was being offered to her, she wasn't sure she liked it.

They left the city, heading south, then west, into cornfields. Red clover, Queen Ann's lace, and chicory bloomed along the roadside. Red, white, and blue, she thought.

"Where are we going?"

"To a family reunion. No reporters, I promise."

"Will I be meeting your parents?"

"No." She caught a hint of strain. Maybe they had liked Marcia. Maybe Meg wasn't— "My aunt and uncle," Cash was saying. "Their branch of the family stayed on the old home place. It was my grandfather and two of his brothers who went out into the world and made a fortune."

"This isn't a political event, then."

"It isn't supposed to be. But you can be sure that my farming cousins will have plenty to say about the PIK program and the drought."

They turned onto a county road. Dust filmed the hood of the car. They passed a neat farm with a windmill and grape arbors out back. Two brown horses cropped grass by the fence. Then the fields closed in again. Jessie would have liked the trip, but Jessie was more and more often with her mother now. Meg traced the long lifeline in Cash's palm. He had not asked where Jessie was. Jonathan would not have forgotten her. Did it matter? They drove another quarter of an hour, the corn giving way to soybeans. Redwing blackbirds swooped along the fencerows. A herd of heavy white clouds grazed on the horizon.

"There," he said.

The farm sat on a small rise, the large white frame house surrounded by shade trees, with a windbreak to the west. The barn and outbuildings were gathered close, giving the farm the self-contained air of a medieval town huddled around its castle. The besieging enemy, Meg knew, was the Illinois winter. Under the trees, where tables and chairs were scattered, and around the long porch of the house, a sizable crowd milled. As they parked in the rutted gravel drive, two young girls trotted by on ponies.

"Third cousins, I think." He took her hand and helped her out of the car. "Ready?"

"I'm not sure. Going to meet the family—all of a sudden that seems pretty serious." She waved a hand. "I didn't mean that the way it sounded."

"Sure you did. It's time you met them, time they met you."

She smiled and broke out in a sweat.

He opened the gate in the picket fence. In the yard Meg saw day lilies, a whiskey barrel planter of petunias, curious faces, a child eating a slice of watermelon and ruining a white sunsuit. Cash squeezed her hand.

A wide-hipped woman with a cast-iron hairdo bustled out of the house, drying her hands on an apron. "There you are, you rascal. I was afraid you'd gotten too important to come and see us."

"Aunt Bea. That's no way to talk about your favorite nephew."

"Oh my, you still give those bear hugs! Well, I guess I shouldn't complain. You do keep in touch. I don't see your mama and daddy unless somebody dies. How are they?" She turned sharp eyes on Meg, then smiled expectantly.

"They're fine. On Martha's Vineyard right now. This is Meg." He looked steadily at his aunt, who pursed her lips and nodded. That seemed to say it all.

Aunt Bea caught Meg in a quick but genuine hug. "I sent Harry down to the cellar for the ice cream freezer. You can meet him later."

"Hey, Congressman, where're your overalls? We're going to get to work after a while!"

Cash hallooed to a group of men in Sunday shirts sitting on straight chairs under the trees.

"Luke and Horace want to ask you about that agricultural census," Aunt Bea explained. "Why don't I take Meg inside and we can get acquainted?" As Meg fell in step with her, she added with a twinkle, "If I have you in the kitchen, all the women will come in out of curiosity. Then we'll have all the kitchen help we need."

"I didn't know I was going to be on exhibit."

"Oh, bless your heart, I don't mean to make you nervous. We're just interested in everything about Cash. We're awful proud of him." They entered a big kitchen crowded with generations of food furniture, from an oak pie safe to a dishwasher in the latest almond shade. "This is Cousin Mae. Mae, this is Meg. She's a friend of Cash's."

Cousin Mae set down the pan of rolls she had taken from the oven and smiled. Meg saw Cash in the width of her mouth and the straightness of the nose.

Aunt Bea put her to work slicing tomatoes, unmolding butter, filling relish dishes. For a while Cash was in the next room, making one phone call after another. Meg wondered if he even knew how to relax. People came and went through the kitchen, as Bea had predicted.

"Take a tater and wait!" Aunt Bea shouted at a boy trying to snitch a drumstick.

"Where did you two meet?" Cousin Mae asked Meg.

"At the school where I work."

"You're a schoolteacher?"

"Sort of. A counselor."

"I wanted to be a schoolteacher," Bea remembered. "But I married Harry and got stuck on this farm, working from kin see to cain't see. Just *had* to get married. Now I wonder what my hurry was. Oh, well!" She handed a platter of fried chicken to a teenage girl who was slipping past. "Shirley, take this outside for me."

Meg watched the reunion through the window over the sink. Now Cash was being questioned by a circle of earnest men. He straddled a chair backward, forearms resting along the back. Often his wit would strike out, convulsing the group. Meg yawned. The kitchen was hot and crowded in a pleasant sort of way. Aunt Bea and Cousin Mae brought more people to meet her. There was general talk about children, weather, other reunions.

She moved over to the kitchen table to cut pies: plum, blackberry, cherry, custard. Cousin Alma caught her looking over her shoulder at the window and laughed. Meg squirmed and everybody laughed.

"I wish I wasn't related to him!" someone declared.

"Not related to whom?" a voice boomed. "You're related to everybody in the county, Phyllis." Cash kissed the woman on the cheek and held out a hand to Meg. "Bea, I'm stealing your kitchen help."

Outside, he filled two plates and they joined a table of Carbondale relatives. "Having a good time?"

"Yes, I am. It was really thoughtful of your aunt to put me in the kitchen, where I could meet people one at a time and feel useful too. She said I'm *almost* as big an attraction as a two-headed calf."

"Yeah, Uncle Harry's the salt of the earth—and Aunt Bea's the pepper."

The meal was interrupted twice by phone calls for Cash. After the second time, he asked a cousin, "Harry doesn't have any of those cordless phones, does he?"

"Are you kidding?"

"Good. Then I'll take Meg on a tour of the farm. But

just to be on the safe side, don't anybody tell where we've gone."

Hand in hand, they strolled to the barnyard, past a shiny green piece of farm machinery that looked to Meg as big as a two-bedroom house.

"I've been coming to these reunions since I was a kid," Cash said. "Used to think I'd be a farmer. In fact, for a long time my mother was scared to death I would." At the fence, a little Jersey raised her nose at them, then went back to chewing her cud. Bees buzzed in a stand of pokeberries.

"Your mother and Marcia are a lot alike?" Meg guessed.

His eyebrows went up. "Quite a leap of intuition. But you're right. Very right."

They passed barn cats sleeping in the sun. Cash picked up a stray ear of corn, shelled it, and tossed the kernels to some chickens. Meg breathed deeply of the many odors: hay, manure, sunbaked vegetation, flowers, chicken feathers. Funny how it always seemed to be high noon in a barnyard, she thought: still, hot, timeless. A scene from childhood flashed on her: herself in a puffy lavender cotton dress and white Mary Janes, sitting cross-legged in clover, sun shining through the hair in her eyes, turning the world to spun gold.

They entered the stuffy darkness of the barn. Something stirred in a stall. In the light from the door, she saw that Cash's face had relaxed.

"Great memories here," he said. "I worked for Uncle Harry my fifteenth and sixteenth summers. Dad wanted to get me away from the life his money had bought. A classic case, I guess: He was nostalgic for what his father had worked so hard to escape. And Uncle Harry straightened out the city boy in a hurry. One day he caught me smoking right here in the barn—*the* unpardonable sin. I found out I wasn't too big to get the daylights whaled out of me."

They climbed the ladder to the loft, Cash in the lead. "And when I was even younger, my cousin Katie and I used to hide from everybody up here." He pulled her down in the hay.

"Not like this, I hope." She let him push her back until she was almost lying down.

Cash stretched out too, his head in her lap. "No, Katie was a tomboy. Her knees were always skinned, and she chipped both front teeth by falling off the roof of the henhouse. Now she's a nurse, with four kids, a ranch house, and a husband with high blood pressure."

"And when she sees her old playmate, they don't have anything to say to each other." She ruffled his hair. "Life."

"At least I've found you." He turned his head and kissed the inside of her elbow.

She leaned back and watched mud daubers building in the eaves. She didn't answer him. There was too much to say.

Up on the drive, car doors slammed. Children's voices streaked through the barnyard and out to the fields. Flies buzzed. The loft ticked and rustled.

Stolen moments are the sweetest, she thought. But will there ever be any other kind for us? "Won't they wonder where we are?"

He yawned, grew heavier on her. "Aunt Bea'll probably figure it out. She knows me. And she's seen you." He chuckled, rolled over, and took her in his arms. "A roll in the hay. Just what the city girl needs."

"Don't you dare!" But when he nibbled her neck, she felt like a filly in a spring meadow. "Hey." She giggled and met his lips eagerly. "Let's stay up here forever."

"Sounds good." His next kiss left her panting. "Meg, the next time there's trouble with my staff or the press, let me know. Don't run off where I can't find you." He kissed the hollow of her throat. "Understand?"

"Mmmm-hmmm." Her skirt slid up her thighs, and

his hand along with it. "This is crazy."

"I know." He undid the top button of her blouse, kissed the creamy rounds of her breasts. She drew his head down, pillowing it there, and held him close. The rise and fall of their breathing found a common rhythm. It was the rhythm of making love. The loft was hot, and they were sweating in their heavy, motionless motion and the hay tickled and she let herself imagine actually making love there... she frowned and shifted her position. All he had to do was grin and there she was, on her back. His eyes were closed. He was probably thinking of something else. Why couldn't she? Because, she mused, there was so little time; and none of it was theirs for certain.

"What happens if you lose?" she asked.

A tic twitched his eyelid. "I've never lost an election, at any level."

"But what if?"

"There's no if. The momentum's swinging my way."

"Surely you've thought about it."

He sat up, serious and calm. "I'd go back to law for a while. But politics is what I'm best at. Come here."

"We're necking like teenagers."

"Better."

Sometime later a voice startled them. "Cash? Cash? Are you in there?"

"That's Great-aunt Julia."

Meg had a wild urge to cackle like a hen. "Should we keep quiet?"

"Nope. She'll send one of her boys up next. I'll see what she wants."

As he started down the ladder, a trembly old voice, now in the barn, said, "Oh there you are. Bea said you might be here."

"What can I do for you, Aunt Julia?"

"Bea says to come on up to the house. They want you

in some pictures; and there's somebody wants to see you."

"Katie? Did she get here after all?"

"No, not Katie."

"I'll be right there."

"Is Meg with you?"

"Yes, she is."

"Well, I don't know. Maybe she shouldn't come."

Cash lowered his voice. "Why not? She's my guest."

"I didn't mean that. I mean you might want to spare her feelings."

"She might as well get used to us now, Aunt Julia. She'll be seeing more of us."

"It isn't us. It's—" A hoarse whisper took over. "Hush, she might hear."

As she descended the ladder, Meg glimpsed the old woman toddling away. "Is anything wrong?"

"She's got a bee in her bonnet about something." He plucked a piece of straw out of her hair. "They probably think I'm being selfish, and they're right. Let's go meet the latecomers. Everybody should have a chance to get to know you."

As they came up to the house, a large group posing for a photographer in front of the hollyhocks chorused, "Cheese."

A bystander said to Cash, "We want Grandpa Joe's descendants next. Wives and children too, in the first picture. Then just the blood relatives."

"Okay." Cash started forward.

"Wait." Meg unhooked her arm from his. "I shouldn't be in these family pictures. Maybe that's what your great-aunt was trying to tell you."

"All right. I'll have Don take one of the two of us after this."

She stood behind the photographer while Cash's group assembled. He shared their strong features and size, but he had been modeled by a different way of life, in which hard physical labor was done in a gym and a good razor cut was more important than the price of corn. As she watched him pose with each arm around a plump cousin, something broke softly inside her, like an egg cracking on the edge of a cup. She wanted to be family, too. His family. Feeling that everyone could read it on her face, she slipped to the kitchen door and inside.

"—didn't need to bring anything, but it was awfully nice of you. It looks real good," Cousin Mae was saying.

"Oh, I wanted to. I haven't forgotten how much Uncle Harry likes angel food cake," Marcia DeWitt replied. She smiled at Meg. "Hello." No sign of recognition.

"Hello." Meg stared, too long. "Uh, can I take that cake out to the dessert table for you?"

"Yes. Thank you." Marcia handed over the cake, her attention sharpening. With her pageboy hairdo, full skirt, and low shoes, she could have stepped straight from the cast of *Oklahoma!* Very smart, Meg thought. She wondered how much of a story her own wilted dress was telling.

"I don't believe we've met. I'm Marcia."

"I'm Meg. I'm a friend of Cash's."

"So am I." Marcia smiled Cash's smile. Maybe they had taken lessons from the same teacher.

Cousin Mae was rattling pans to beat the band.

"I'll bet you can tell me where he is." Marcia smiled again.

Meg enjoyed the thought of grinding the cake into Marcia's lovely face. "Outside."

Voices came from under the open window. The screen door creaked. Aunt Bea came in with Cash.

"Oh, mercy. Why, Marcia. How are you?" Bea fluttered, as if she didn't already know Marcia had arrived.

"Aunt Bea." Marcia kissed her on both cheeks.

Maybe Meg could just tip the plate and let the cake slide off...

Marcia moved over to Cash, tilting a cheek up for a kiss. "Hi, C.D."

His lips brushed the peachy skin. He flushed deeply. If she threw the cake now, she could get them both...

"I wonder if we could talk privately," Marcia said with quiet assurance, as if they were already alone.

"Maybe. What's it about?"

She paused, with an actress's timing. "Winning."

"Did Sam send you?"

"It was my idea, too." She brushed at a cobweb on his shoulder. "Playing farmer again?"

He frowned. "We can talk outside. Meg?"

"Sure. Go ahead."

Aunt Bea pressed Meg's hand. "Let's take that cake out and see where my daughter-in-law has gotten to. I want to show you my new grandson."

New little Todd spit up on Meg's shoulder as soon as he was handed to her.

Marcia and Cash paced a strip of grass on the other side of the drive, next to a soybean field. In the yard, the relatives clotted in twos and threes, talking about them. Cash's head was bent, his brows knitted. From time to time, Marcia touched him lightly on the arm. She did the talking. He weighed every word she said.

Meg turned her chair so that her back was to them. The women at her table were comparing fabric softeners. Aunt Bea had disappeared. Meg remembered the furniture that Marcia had left in the Georgetown apartment. Maybe she'd always intended to come back to it.

The woman holding Todd on her lap suddenly thrust him out at arm's length. "He's wet."

"I'll change him," Meg said. "I don't mind."

Todd's mother rolled her eyes in gratitude. "Would you? Everything's in the front bedroom."

The kid was a kicker. Changing his diaper was like putting socks on an octopus. In the dresser mirror, Meg mimicked herself, "I don't mind."

When she got back outside, Cash and Marcia were gone. Cousin Hazel passed her, smiling apologetically. The sun was at three o'clock. Under it, the farm was baking like a pie. On the side steps of the porch, men in shirtsleeves crowded around a portable radio, listening to a ballgame. Children fought over the tire swing. Every person there knew more about Cash than she did.

He loomed silently beside her.

"Where's Marcia?" she asked.

"Gone. I need to get back to town."

"Problems?"

"No, I hadn't planned to stay much longer. I have to give an after-dinner speech in Hadley tonight. Is that okay with you?"

"Anything's fine with me." In the car, she said, "Everyone was very kind."

"Too kind. They were embarrassed." He squinted through the cloud that a car ahead of them had kicked up. Eating Marcia's dust, Meg thought. "I'm sorry," he said.

"Am I allowed to ask what she wanted?"

He flexed his fingers on the steering wheel. "She wanted to come back to me. For political reasons."

"Tell me another one."

"Sam thinks it'll clinch the election."

"Why should she care?"

"She owes me. She owes her father. And she loves to campaign."

"No, I'll tell you why," Meg said. "Because she knows she made a mistake when she let you go. She wants you back, politics be damned."

"That isn't it." He lowered his head. She thought of a bull backed into a chute. "She's offering joint public appearances, not remarriage. We'd go our separate ways later. It's been done before."

"I seem to remember your refusing to live a lie back in June. But I guess the thirst for power must corrupt as absolutely as the actual possession of it."

His right hand came off the steering wheel fast, as if he were going to hit her. He ran it roughly through his hair. "You're on dangerous ground."

"I'd say *you* are, if you think your marriage is the deciding factor in the campaign. Don't you people ever address the issues, for heaven's sake?"

He seemed to grow larger. She imagined him turning green and bursting out of his shirt like the Incredible Hulk. "It's you who has the distorted perspective," he shot back. "Saunders and I know what the important issues are, and we keep hammering away at them. All you can see is what's going to happen between you and me."

She fumed, fighting for control. She lost. "Well, how do you like having two women after you?"

"I didn't know she was going to be here. If you're jealous, it's your problem."

"And of course you never get jealous. The upper classes never do. Not part of their value system."

"Yes, I get jealous, Meg. Whenever and wherever I want to. Your problem is that you go around pretending to be 'liberated' and 'understanding,' but you cave in the minute anybody looks at your man, just like anybody else would. And it makes you mad. The sooner you admit you're human, the better."

You Neanderthal, she thought. "I care about you as a person! I don't want to see you lose, but if you did, it wouldn't change the way I feel about you. And if this race is going to affect your morals, twist your character—"

"That's enough!" he bellowed.

She shut up for good.

When he pulled up in front of her apartment, she threw open the door.

He reached across her and closed it. "I turned her down."

"But you considered it."

"No."

"I'm glad." *You did, you did, you did,* she insisted silently. *I can see it in your eyes.*

"I'm going to be on the road for the next two weeks," he said, "but we'll get together." He leaned over to kiss her, but she slid away and got out of the car.

Eyes brimming with tears, she said, "I wish I didn't love you."

When she got upstairs, she looked out the window. The big black car was just moving off, slowly.

By the next day, rumors of a Delaney reconciliation were in the newspapers.

CHAPTER EIGHT

JONATHAN SET THE arm of the stereo down with tedious care, and Billie Holliday started "Lover Man." He nodded and came back to the couch.

"I really appreciate your coming over tonight," Meg said. She finished the tenth row of stockinette and reversed the needles. "Thursday nights are the pits." Jonathan nodded again, but she explained anyway, "Jessie came to me on a Thursday, and she went back home on a Thursday."

"How's that working out?"

"Okay, so far. Karen's doing well at her job and has a good sitter lined up until school starts. She's marrying Timmy's father next month. He's been the only man in her life for a long time now. Jessie likes him." Meg half smiled. "Yesterday Jess called to see how *I* was doing."

Jonathan shelled more pistachios, then popped them in his mouth. "Are you going to take another child?"

"Not soon. This has been a pretty emotional experience." She counted rows. "Eventually, yes, I'd like to have another child with me. And I'll know not to get so involved next time. Besides, once you get on the list, the agency won't let you alone."

Billie slid into "What a Little Moonlight Can Do."

Jonathan said, "Jessie filled a particular void in your life. You probably won't ever need anybody that badly again."

"You don't think so?"

He mused. "No. The affection you gave each other made both of you stronger. That won't go away."

"What a sweet thing to say." She patted his shoulder. "You're a good friend. I hope you and I have helped each other, too."

"You don't need me enough."

The edge of bitterness to his voice caught her off guard. Jonathan was never bitter. Carefully, she said, "I need a friend, and we agreed to be just friends."

"I know. We could have gone on that way a long time." He emptied the bowl of nutshells into the wastebasket beside the couch. He was stalling, and they both knew it. Tension hummed in the air. "But things have changed."

"I'm not sure they have." She glanced his way, waited. "You're too polite to ask."

"Maybe I don't want to know." Pain had replaced the bitterness.

"Jonathan, I'm not trying to make you jealous. I didn't even think I could."

He looked at her very straight. She felt helpless.

"I haven't heard from Cash in two weeks," she said quietly. "And you've read the papers, same as I have. But I think we should be talking about you. Um—how about another cup of tea?"

"I should be going."

"Jonathan, please don't run away from this. I feel so stupid, so blind. I never meant to hurt you."

He polished his glasses on his shirttail. Without them,

he looked like one of the lesser apostles, only more understanding. "Things have changed inside you, Meg, no matter what his feelings are. That's why there's no room for me in your life now." He got to his feet. "No, that's not quite fair. You've always had a faraway look in your eyes; and you've been straight with me about that. I was the one who tried to make more out of our relationship than was there."

"Jonathan..." She followed him to the door. "I'm sorry."

"For what?"

"Everything. We should have talked more about feelings, and much earlier. I didn't realize you—" She sighed and spread her hands.

"Neither did I, for a long time. Not until Delaney came into your life. Don't worry about it. I'll live." He kissed her cheek. "Bye."

"But can we still be friends? Or would it be too painful for you? I'll do whatever—" She choked.

"Sure." He smiled tiredly. "Want a ride to the workshop tomorrow?"

Heavy footsteps toiled up the stairs.

"Yes. We'll talk more." She hugged him, patting his back. "Thanks. For being such a wonderful guy."

"Good evening," Cash said, coming down the hall, his shadow leaping ahead of him.

Meg let go of Jonathan in slow motion.

All Zen cool, Jonathan stuck out his hand. "Evening."

"It's Jonathan, isn't it?"

"That's right."

A noise came from behind Ruth's door, opposite them.

"Shall we go inside?" Meg suggested.

Nobody moved.

"Campaign keep you pretty busy?" Jonathan asked mildly, but the hand with which he zipped his jacket trembled slightly.

"Yeah. It's been rough." Cash checked his watch. He

hadn't looked at Meg yet. "Didn't think I'd make it home tonight, even." He appeared dazed.

"Well, *I'm* going in," Meg said, and did. She sat down on the couch, out of their view, and buried her face in her hands.

Somebody shut the door to the hall. Muffled voices went back and forth. She knew she was crying when tears hit her knees. Wiping her eyes, she realized Jonathan was saying, "Meg... hurt..." She jumped up and threw open the door.

Jonathan was disappearing down the stairs, not hurrying.

Cash was facing her, his hand reaching for the doorknob.

She wheeled back to the couch and collapsed on it, sobbing.

After what seemed like a long time, the door closed. The couch sagged as Cash sat down on the other end of it. "Here." He held out a folded handkerchief.

"Thanks." She patted her face with it and went on crying.

After a while, he said, "Blow your nose."

"I can't blow my nose. I don't know how."

"Do it."

"I'm afraid I'll blow my brains out."

He laughed tiredly, rested his head on the back of the couch, and closed his eyes. In a little while the church bell on Seventh Avenue tolled midnight.

Meg hiccuped twice, and her crying trailed off. Cash didn't move. She inched closer to him. He was sound asleep. There were dark circles under his eyes, and his skin was gray from exhaustion. A fallen hero, she thought, edging off the couch. He opened his eyes. She sat down again.

"What a hell of a mess," he said to the floor.

"I wasn't crying for you. I was crying because I've hurt Jonathan."

"Believe me, I don't deserve your tears."

"And Jessie's gone back to her mother."

His shoulders sagged. "I should have been here."

"And I'm tired. My heart is tired."

Cash leaned forward, forearms on thighs, hands hanging between his knees. His head was down. "It was going to be just another affair," he said slowly. "The best one of all, but still, good-bye was built into the hello. You knew it, of course. That's why you kept pushing for my motives, kept fighting me."

"I didn't fight hard enough."

He eyed her sideways, then went back to staring down. "I've told myself for years that I wasn't hurting anybody, that you couldn't hurt my brand of hard-shelled woman with a Mack truck. But I did hurt some of them. Now I've hurt you. Maybe the rest of them got what they expected. But your—hurting you is different."

She refolded his handkerchief. "Did Jonathan tell you this?"

"He didn't tell me anything I didn't already know."

The record player clicked off.

She said, "There's a lot of pain going around. Maybe I would have hurt Jonathan anyway. But not this soon and not this way. I think of myself as an honest person, but I haven't been honest with him since the day you came to Ingersoll School." She gripped her knees and looked straight ahead. "My fault entirely. I don't blame you."

He was silent for so long that she thought he'd fallen asleep again. Then he said tentatively, "How've you been?"

"The telephone was invented in 1876. You could have called."

The phone in the kitchen rang. Neither of them laughed. Meg answered it.

A masculine voice she didn't recognize asked for Congressman Delaney.

Cash's eyes were closed again. His legs were propped on the coffee table, and his arms were draped loosely along the back of the couch. She'd never seen anyone look so beat. "I believe you have the wrong number."

When she went back to the living room, she took with her the newspaper clipping she'd taped to the door of the refrigerator. Cash looked up, and she handed it to him. "I assume this is the reason I haven't heard from you."

Cash and Marcia standing on a podium, hands held high in victory. Marcia with those plastically perfect proportions that only Eleanor Roosevelt, among political wives, had ever escaped. Cash looking like he'd just been elected president of the universe, his American flag lapel pin flashing in the sun. Caption: AIRPORT RECONCILIATION. Date: eight days earlier.

The phone rang again.

Cash tossed the picture in the wastebasket. "I'm here to tell you why I haven't phoned." He yawned, scoured his face with a palm.

"When was the last time you got any sleep?"

"Day before yesterday. Four hours. Before that, I can't remember. I had to make an unexpected trip to Washington because of that Cuban development."

The phone stopped ringing.

"Go home and go to bed," she said.

"No. I've waited too long as it is. Listen to me. That picture was taken when I flew in from Taylor. A big crowd was waiting, which should have tipped me off. Nobody meets my plane on those short hops. She joined me while I was greeting them. The way the press is watching my personal life, there was nothing to do but go along with it for the moment. I can't afford another public skirmish with a woman."

"So I was supposed to sit quietly at home and wait for you to turn up with an explanation. And heaven help me, I have. Here we are: You're talking, I'm listening."

She got up to pace. "You've pushed me back into old victim patterns I thought I'd outgrown. Do you know what I found myself wondering just last week? Whether it was better to be the equal of an ordinary man or the mere plaything of an extraordinary one." She laughed harshly. "I must be losing my mind."

"A truly extraordinary man would never present you with that option." He hunched his shoulders. "I didn't call you because of the publicity surrounding this trouble with Marcia. The press is on my tail every second, and that phone call just now was probably one of them. I didn't want you drawn into this. You'd be cut to ribbons by the DeWitt interests. And I wanted you to be able to say honestly that you hadn't heard from me, if you were asked."

"Couldn't you have sent a carrier pigeon? Or does the press birdwatch too?" She was at the window now, her back to him.

His voice got louder, harder. "The reason behind the reason I didn't call is this: I couldn't handle your falling in love with me."

She looked out into the black sky. "You know I always take responsibility for my mistakes. Falling in love with you is one of them. It isn't your problem. Besides, I'm working on reversing the process."

"Yeah, that's the way I've always handled it before— take what I want and let the lady look out for herself. But not this time. This time we share the responsibility. Because I'm in love with you, too."

Very slowly, she turned around. "Then everything makes less sense, not more." Her tears had dried like glue, masking her face with calm. Inside her, a marimba band was getting drunk.

"I haven't told you all of it." He patted the couch. She sat down, a little nearer to him than before. He looked more tired than when he had arrived. "I've broken with DeWitt and his machine. I'm all alone now." His mouth twisted wryly. "Except for the people."

"When?"

"Today. Marcia's stunt brought it all to a head, but there's been trouble for some time. I'm too much my own man to suit them." He shrugged. "It'll hit the papers tomorrow. Then we'll see if I've committed political suicide or not. The smart money says yes."

"Do you care?"

"Of course I care."

"I had to ask, since you've apparently done something deliberately self-destructive."

"It had to be done."

"But why didn't you wait until after the election?"

He shook his head savagely. "I'm nobody's show horse. They asked too much, asked for deals I'm not willing to make. It's not a good time to get out, but it's time. And another thing: I didn't do anything illegal during my association with him, so I'm not afraid to face the voters on my own. My stands on the issues have always been mine, so I won't be changing my tune."

The phone started ringing again. Meg got up and put it in the refrigerator. "Does this mean staff changes?"

"Some. Fortunately, most of my best people are standing by me."

"Brenda?"

"Yes. But maybe not for the right reasons. I had a long talk with her last night, straightened some things out. I think she'll be all right."

"You're certainly putting your house in order. I'm proud of you, Cash, more than I can say. I always knew you had high principles. But I thought—"

"You thought I expected *other* people to live up to them?"

"Yes." They rode out a testy silence. Then she said, "I still don't understand why so much of this campaign centers on personalities. I expected Ted to run a cleaner show."

"Not me?"

"I didn't know what to expect from you."

"I'll tell you why my personal life has become an issue. Because Saunders is waffling on some of the major issues. In the beginning, he took some positions that were so far left of say, George McGovern, that they weren't even in sight. Now he's modifying those. His staff is smart enough to swing the spotlight elsewhere."

"Ted Saunders is a nice man."

"You know where nice guys finish, don't you?"

"Are you saying you aren't a nice guy?" she asked.

"I'm a good guy. It's not the same thing."

She picked up her knitting.

"Who's the sweater for?" he asked.

"My brother."

"I didn't know you had a brother."

"There's a lot you don't know about me." She said it without heat.

He took it that way. "There's a lot you don't know about me, either."

"Then can I ask you something?"

"Shoot."

"Remember the first time you came here and we went to the Fern Bar? Afterward, in the kitchen, you were giving me a big rush, and I was resisting. And then you looked at the clock and suddenly decided to pack it in. After you'd gone, Brenda called from your place. So I figured you went home to her. Was I right?"

"Not home to sleep with her. There's never been anything between Brenda and me except business. Sometimes she's too caught up in her job, and she was that night. No, I left for another reason. The clock had nothing to do with it." His hand hovered over hers and withdrew. "There's something about you, Meg, that makes me examine myself more closely than I sometimes want to. It's not so much what you say as it is the attitude you project. You're a good person. Cheap things shouldn't happen to you. That night, in the kitchen, I suddenly saw the situation from your point of view. It's never happened to me before, that kind of empathy. I was pushing too hard, was even frightening you a little. So I backed off."

"You don't even have a reverse gear," she tried to tease.

"I tried to wait for you to catch up with me."

"It didn't take me long." She unwound some yarn.

"No need to go into that." He stood up. "I'll be leaving now."

"You'll what?"

"I said what I came to say. I'll call you tomorrow." He lumbered toward the door.

When he got there, she was standing in front of it. "Cash, we're being entirely too adult about this."

He halted, swaying slightly.

"Are you all right?"

"Just need some sleep." He motioned her out of the way.

"But you just said you're in love with me."

"Yep. And I still will be tomorrow."

"You can't tell me something like that and then just walk out."

"You expect me to demand payment? Then you haven't been listening."

"No, you big idiot, I expect you to stay and let me take care of you. You're exhausted." She wrapped her arms around him and braced for a struggle. "Besides, I'll bet there's nothing for breakfast at your house."

"Contrary to what women think, men can take care of themselves."

"This is no time to prove it. Come on."

In the bedroom, she turned down the covers and pointed. "In you go. No argument."

He managed a shadow of his famous smile. "For the first time in my argumentative life, I can't think of an argument. And what are you going to do?"

"I'm going to get you some warm milk."

"Scotch or nothing."

"I'll see if there is any."

"You do that. Then figure out what we're going to do next."

But when she came back after five minutes of rummaging through cabinets, with an inch of Irish whiskey over ice, he was sound asleep with the light on. She sat down on the edge of the bed. He lay on his back, naked under the sheet. The mat of hair on his chest caught the light with the rise and fall of his breathing. He needed a shave. Even in sleep he looked stubborn, with his squarish chin tilted up to show a short, deep scar on the underside.

Meg removed her cutoffs and panties, leaving on the roomy *M.A.S.H.* T-shirt, then sat down again, a pillow between the headboard and her shoulder blades. She sipped the smoky liquid and tried to remember where the bottle had come from. A man? A party? No luck.

Cash sighed, moved his lips.

She resisted the impulse to kiss him. What did he mean when he said he loved her? For her, truth was something solid and pure, like a block of gold. She had the idea that Cash dealt in alloys of truth. And what did it mean that he had showed up on her doorstep in this condition? She put down the glass and took the pins out of her hair. But she knew the answer to that one. He needed her. For now, maybe that should be enough. She drank some more and rubbed the cold glass across her forehead. So this is the private Cash Delaney, she thought. She turned out the light and stretched out on her side. The whiskey lay on her brain like satin. She slept.

In the night he came to her.

She drifted up through layers of sleep to find herself lying in the middle of the bed, a heavy, bearish warmth nudging her backside. His arm lay over her, his hand curled between her breasts. She stretched and instantly came alive to his contours. He rolled her over, pulling her shirt up and off. He wrapped his powerful legs around her, crushing her to him. They kissed and touched. She moaned softly and struggled, because struggling felt good. She touched his lips with her fingertips. He was smiling. He rolled onto his back, pulling her on top of him. It was like lying on a mountain range.

"And I just intended to pay a social call," he mumbled.

"Would you like a cup of tea? Crumpets?"

"No, this is just fine." He raised his head, kissed her breasts. Then he lay back down, fingering the nipples to make them stand up. She could see him dimly in the city glow from the window, and he her. He pulled her hair over her breasts, then divided it so the nipples peaked out.

"Lady Godiva."

"And look what I'm riding."

Gently, he lifted her hips, then let her down, sliding inside her.

Her nails dug into his shoulders. "So deep..."

He began to move slowly, maybe teasing a little, but each time quicker and, incredibly, deeper. The end of each thrust made her cry out; then suddenly it was all pleasure. Her lips, hot and moist, roamed his chest and shoulders. Dizzy with need, she moved with him until, with a tremendous upheaval, still joined, they rolled again and he was above her, driving faster and faster until she was shuddering out of control, and she screamed and felt tears on her cheeks and held on through the shattering, tearing entrance into wonder.

When the room stopped spinning, she touched his face and found that the tears were his.

"I love you, Meg," he growled. "Dammit, I do."

She woke up smelling burned butter. The clock radio showed an uncivilized hour. She sniffed again and detected meltdown of her no-stick skillet. "Good morning," she called.

"Morning. Breakfast in five minutes."

"I'll be there."

She showered, threw on white shorts and a pink T-shirt without a message on it, and brushed out her hair.

In the kitchen doorway, she stopped cold. "My, you've been busy."

The sink was piled high with dirty mixing bowls and utensils. Two platters of pancakes sat on the counter. A plate of pancakes waited on the breakfast table, in addition to the stacks on each of their plates. There was a small puddle of batter on the floor. It had gotten there by running down the cabinets from a larger puddle on the counter.

Cash was at the stove, turning out more of the little devils. "There's sausage, too," he said.

She began to laugh. He turned and looked at her with an utterly blank curiosity, like a stag seeing its first automobile. "What's the matter with you?"

"Nothing, not a thing." She leaned against the doorjamb, whooping. "It's... it's just so"—her shoulders shook—"nice to have you here."

"Hope you're hungry."

She looked at the spread of pancakes. That set her off again.

"Here." He handed her a mug of coffee. "Sober up."

"Last night I thought I'd be nursing you back to health for a month. But this A.M. you look totally restored."

"You're the best medicine there is," he said, pouring hot syrup from pan to pitcher.

Meg tucked a swallow of coffee behind her teeth and then knocked it back fast, the way she'd been taught to drink moonshine. Even so, she tasted it; it was just as strong as before. She carried her cup to the breakfast table and poured in milk. Amazingly, it didn't curdle.

Cash turned off the stove and came over to her. He

put his arms around her. "All I need is you, babe. I knew if I got here and saw you, I'd be all right." He kissed her hair. "You're not going to jump on me for calling you babe?"

"I guess if I could mother you last night, you can baby me this morning."

They sat down to eat.

"Good pancakes," she noted. "Nice and light."

"Guess my cook was right. Club soda makes a difference."

"I don't have any club soda."

"The all-night grocery on Ninth does."

"You've already been out?"

He nodded, absorbed in his meal. "Wanted to get the morning edition of the *Gazette*, but I was too early. I'm ready to fight again."

Meg put down her fork, propped her chin on her knuckles, and studied him. He was eating like a lumberjack, and he looked like one: His eyes sparkled, the whites clear and bluish; his complexion under the stubble was outdoors-ruddy; his shoulders, beneath the wrinkled dress shirt, looked like a shelf of granite. She could hardly believe he was the same man of the evening before.

"About what I said last night," he began without looking up.

"Here it comes."

"I meant it." He cut into his second sausage. "About loving you."

She said nothing, but it finally sank in.

"I hope you still feel that way about me." He reached for the butter.

"Yes. Only..."

"Only what?"

"I'm like the dog that chases cars," she said. "Now that I've caught one, what do I do with it?"

"You weren't at a loss last night." He grinned broadly, pleased with them both.

It was impossible not to grin back. "Seriously, Cash. I'm overwhelmed. Humbled. But what does it mean?"

"What does it mean?" He shook his head. "If I said good morning to you, you'd ask me to define the nature of goodness. Know what the trouble with you social workers is? You're too careful with your emotions. I'm not talking about love measured out in teaspoonfuls. I mean all of it."

"Oh. Well. So do I."

Then it really sank in.

He pushed back his chair and held out his arms in that way she knew so well. Instantly, she was on his lap, squeezing him as hard as she could. "Hey"—he chuckled—"that's more like it." After a bit, he added, "Let's just hang on until after the election. Then we can make plans." He moved his head, and she knew he was looking at the clock.

"Do you have to go?" she asked.

"Soon."

"But the hearts and flowers haven't arrived. The violins are still tuning up."

"When it's real, you don't need them," he said.

"You're right. Mr. Right, in fact."

"I need to call a cab."

She got off his lap so he could. He did and then took her face in his hands. "Damn if I don't hear music every time I look at you, anyway."

She stood on tiptoe and kissed his cheek. "When will I see you again?"

"I'll call."

"I've heard that before."

"Every night."

And he did.

CHAPTER NINE

"AND SO," THE commentator concluded, "Delaney's open break with the powerful Samuel E. DeWitt has turned out to be the masterstroke of this political campaign. In early trouble with the voters of Masefield for his conservative stands on defense spending and domestic policy, Delaney now seems virtually unbeatable in his bid for reelection. Without modifying his deeply held conservative views, he has garnered support among moderates and even some liberals by his opposition to what he has labeled the 'back room brand' of downstate politics. Analysts this morning generally agree that in last night's televised debate with opponent Ted Saunders, a Masefield lawyer, Delaney emerged the clear winner, despite a heated exchange over Delaney's past political associations. After the debate, a member of Saunders's staff stated, 'We knew it wouldn't be easy, and we haven't given up the fight.' Mr. DeWitt continues to refuse comment on the new direction of his former son-in-law's campaign, as does C.J. Delaney, Senior, the congressman's father and frequent contributor to conservative causes. In a moment I'll return w—"

Meg cut the VW's engine and radio. Students streamed across the parking lot toward the open doors of Ingersoll School. Most of them looked happy and eager; it was only the second week of the new school year. As she joined them she saw, in the tall window on the second-floor landing of the school building, a rotund figure watching the flow of children. When Mr. Stanley, the principal, saw her, he motioned to her.

"Morning," he greeted her a few moments later, at the head of the stairs. "I saw your friend on television last night. Pretty impressive, I'll have to admit."

Meg dimpled. "He was, wasn't he?"

They walked down the hall to Meg's office, student exuberance waning at the principal's approach.

"You know Delaney pretty well, do you?" Mr. Stanley asked.

"Pretty well." Meg unlocked her door, and they went in.

"See him often?"

"We keep in touch." She put her purse in a drawer. "Would you like me to give him a message?"

"No, no." Mr. Stanley rattled keys in his pocket and moved the chair in front of Meg's desk a couple of inches to the right. "No, I wanted to see you about something else." He handed her a manila folder.

Meg read the name on the tab. "Paul Ward? I don't know him."

"He's a new student, a junior. I'd like you to have a talk with him."

"What's the problem?"

"He's been in three fights since school started. Yesterday afternoon on the bus he broke a boy's glasses and bloodied his nose. He also broke some equipment in the science lab on Monday, playing a prank. He talks back and is generally disrespectful. He's already a regular in detention."

"What kind of student is he? As if I didn't know."

"Poor. But he has an IQ of a hundred forty-three. Unbelievable, considering his background."

"How about his family?"

"He's been in foster care most of his life."

"Any trouble outside of school?"

"Mostly truancy. About six months ago, he hot-wired a car and got caught returning it after a joyride."

"Drugs?"

"I'd expect it, but there's nothing in his records."

Meg sat down at her desk. "What do you want me to do?"

"For now, just establish contact. He's got a lot bottled up inside. He need to talk to somebody. He's high-risk to get into big trouble, in my view."

"Do you think he'll talk to me?"

"You always get them to talk, don't you? He's in my office. I'll send him down." He paused at the door. "I'll be interested to hear what you think of some things he says."

While she waited, Meg straightened her desk and thought about the debate. Cash's intelligence was formidable. She didn't agree with half of what he said, but that was mostly out of stubbornness. She'd have to think up some better defenses for her opinions before she saw him on Thursday. On Thursday it would be two weeks since he had come to her exhausted. Two weeks since he'd admitted his feelings for her. Maybe the most contented two weeks of her life, even though they'd been apart.

"Hey, fox."

Paul Ward was tall and skinny. He'd have to stand in one place a long time to cast a shadow. Thick black hair, curly and uncombed. Pale skin. Mean, dark eyes.

"Come in, Paul." Meg was friendly but professional.

"My name is Meg. I don't answer to anything else. Would you please close the door?"

Jeans. Old, but somebody had cared enough to iron them. Cheap satin jacket, frayed at the cuffs. On the back, an appliquéd top hat and cane to illustrate the legend THE SOPHISTICATES. He shambled to a chair, sprawled in it, and put his feet up on the corner of her desk. Beat-up Weejuns with the heels run over. He sneered at her, dared her to make something of it.

"Paul, I understand you're new here. Where did you move from?"

"You've got my record, fox."

"I haven't read it. And I don't like to be called names."

He slouched down on his tailbone and looked out the window across the room. "You're really on top of things, aren't you, fox?"

"I haven't read it, turkey, because I want to hear what you have to say about yourself."

"Nothing."

"I'd guess you're from the St. Louis area, by your accent."

Paul Ward folded his arms and went on looking out the window. Meg let him have his fun for a while. Silence could cut both ways.

Then she said, "Moving to a new city can be upsetting. But when you're sixteen, you've got to go where the family goes."

They sat some more. "Not for much longer," Paul said suddenly.

"Yes, soon you'll be on your own." She straightened the desk blotter. "What are your plans?"

He shrugged jerkily. "Go to college."

Surprise, surprise. "Any special course of study?"

Two spots of color sprang up on his cheeks. "Engineering."

"That's fine, Paul. I've been told you have the ability

to be anything you want to be. But your record might not be good enough to get in. You have to think about the requirements."

He scratched around in his hair and transferred his gaze to the brass paperweight on her desk. "Yeah well, my dad'll have something to say about that, maybe."

"I don't think your parents can help you if you haven't done the work."

Finally, he looked at her. His eyes were crafty—and something else too. "You don't know who my father is. My real father."

"Suppose you tell me."

"It's that congressman. That Cash Delaney."

It was dark that evening when Meg parked beside the Continental on the back side of the Ramada Inn in Telford City. She went up to the second level of the motel and knocked on the door of number 214.

A burly man opened it. Cigarette smoke and laughter blasted out around him. "Yes?" He exuded solid midwestern prosperity and sandy good looks that were eroded around the eyes. She'd seen him somewhere before, but not in person.

"Is Cash—?"

"Meg!" Cash heaved himself out of a chair and in a stride was at the threshold, hugging her off her feet. Then he swung her around and introduced her to the handful of men in the room. The doorman's name, Joe Ignasiak, identified him as a former Chicago Bears quarterback, now a popular figure in state politics.

"I was hoping you'd have a few minutes, Cash," she said, her face hot.

"Sure. I've got about an hour before I have to give a speech."

"You seem to be busy. I don't want to break up the party."

"It's okay. Guys, we can finish this later." Cash saw them through the connecting door to the next room and closed it behind them. Then he grinned at her, hands on hips. "What a great surprise."

"I hope you really don't mind. I guess I should have called first. That short man didn't look happy to see me."

"But I am." He caught her in a bear hug, burying his face in her neck.

She bent away from him, laughing. "That tickles!" The edge of the bed caught her behind the knees. She toppled backward, Cash on top of her.

He stopped her giggles with a kiss. "Caught you."

"This isn't what I came here for."

"Liar. Boy, I've missed you."

She struggled up on her elbows. "Those men in the next room."

"What about them?"

"They'll hear."

"Then keep quiet." He grinned and kissed her again. Then he quit kidding and let her go. "Okay. I know you well enough to know you didn't come here just to cheer me up."

Why was she always the one who stopped the fun? She played with the buttons on his shirt. "I do need to talk to you about something."

"First, can you stay the night?"

"Congressman, I do believe you have a one-track mind."

"True. I've been thinking of nothing but the campaign twenty-four hours a day. Cramming for the debate took care of my spare time. I'm ready to switch tracks."

"You were grand last night." Meg smiled. "It's times like that, when I see you on television, that I can't believe I actually know you."

"But you're my debate coach." He grinned. "It was all that arguing with you that sharpened me up for Saunders. After you, he was a piece of cake." He patted her hand and moved to a chair.

"Cash, you know it wouldn't be practical for me to stay the night."

"Yeah, babe, but I wish you could be out on the road with me. Maybe we can work out something for the next campaign."

"Maybe." Two years away? He was thinking that far ahead for them?

"Say," he went on with energy, "I met the seven o'clock shift at the tractor plant this morning, and the comments on the debate were really good."

"I think all you have to do is stay alive until Election Day. You're a shoo-in."

"How's school going?" he asked.

"Fine. But that's what I want to talk to you about, in a way." She scooted off the bed, went around behind him, and massaged his shoulders. "I had a sixteen-year-old boy in my office today, a troublemaker. Mr. Stanley thinks I can help him straighten out."

"I thought you worked with younger kids."

"I get all ages. Ingersoll is one of the last twelve-grade neighborhood schools left in Masefield." She worked on a knot of tension in his right shoulder. "I don't suppose the name Paul Ward means anything to you."

"No. A little more to the right. Ah, yes. There."

"I didn't think it would. He has the last name Ward because he was a ward of the state from birth. A nurse named him Paul after her brother."

"Is he a real problem to you?" Cash asked. "I don't understand what I can do to help."

"He says he's your son."

Cash lowered his head. "Left now. Good. You drove all the way down here to tell me that?"

"Well, yes. I thought it was important. Isn't it? He

wasn't teasing me. He doesn't even know that I know you. He's serious. And it's affecting his sense of identity."

"How many people know about this?" Cash asked.

"Just Mr. Stanley and me, as far as I know, and probably his foster parents. I think Paul's smart enough to realize that the other kids would ridicule him if he spread the story around. Aren't you going to do anything about it?"

"Meg, Meg." Cash shook his head. "I appreciate your concern. But when you've been around politics as long as I have, you learn to ignore all these crackpots. They just want attention."

She sat down on the chair arm. "Do a lot of people claim to be your son?"

"No, of course not. But you'd be surprised at the lengths to which some people will go in order to establish a personal connection with a 'celebrity.' Most of it is harmless. Once in a while somebody has to be cooled off. Just consider this: The boy is sixteen years old. Why is he just now claiming to be my son? Because I'm in the news a lot right now, that's why. He's probably a mixed-up kid who's created his own genealogy to make himself feel more important. The worst thing I could do for him would be to give his fantasy credibility by dealing with it."

"Maybe," Meg said. "It couldn't possibly be true?"

"No."

"But, Cash, he believes it, with all his heart. That's what makes it so pathetic."

"How does he 'know' he's my son?"

"He says he received a letter about a month ago, telling him."

"Anonymous, I'll bet."

"Yes."

Cash snorted. "Cruel. Poor kid. You said he was a ward of the state. Where does he live?"

"He's been in foster care for a long time now. He had heart trouble as a youngster and that kept him from being adopted until he simply got past the prime age. Not many people want to take on a surly teenager, especially a boy. He's had a rough life, and it hasn't been his fault."

"What about his heart?"

"He had surgery a few years ago. He's okay now."

Cash stood and stretched. "Well, sorry I can't help you on this, babe. I'd say your best bet is to discuss it with his foster family."

"I guess you're right. I should get to know them. They're new in town."

"Where from?"

"Near Granite City. The father lost his job, and they were running out of money when he got an offer here, about a month ago."

"About a month ago." Cash looked thoughtful. Someone tapped on the connecting door. "Come in."

Joe Ignasiak stuck his head in. "We're tired of rubber chicken. Want a burger before the banquet? I'm going out for some."

"Meg?"

"No thanks."

"I'll pass, Joe. Guess what Meg has been telling me? Some high school boy in Masefield is claiming to be my son. Not true, by the way."

"Terrific. Just what the campaign needs." Joe came into the room. "He isn't talking to reporters, is he?"

"No," Meg put in. "That is, I don't think so."

"Don't think so!" Joe slammed a fist into his palm. "Is this some trick of Saunders?"

"No, it wouldn't be," Cash said. "Ted isn't running that kind of campaign. That's one good thing about running against an idealist."

"You know the kid?" Joe asked Meg.

"I'm his school counselor."

"See what you can do to make him forget it, okay?"

He clapped Cash on the shoulder. "This cat only has nine lives, and he's used up several already, living down the divorce, the break with DeWitt—"

"Me," Meg added.

Joe looked uncomfortable. "That too. An illegitimate son wouldn't help at this point. It's less than two months till Election Day."

"But it isn't true," Meg reminded him.

"It wouldn't have to be," Joe replied, "if the wrong people got hold of it. Proving it's not true would take longer than we've got."

"Relax," Cash told them. "The boy may already have abandoned the idea. Maybe he just needed a little leverage to get out of a tight spot with his counselor. Is everything set at the VFW?"

He and Joe discussed it. Meg shifted from one foot to the other. Why was she bothering him about a heartbreak kid? Cash was totally absorbed by the battle and the coming victory. She couldn't blame him, yet she was disappointed. "I'd better be going," she announced.

Cash walked her to the car. "I'm glad you came, Meg. But you understand my position on this Paul Ward thing?"

"Yes. I guess I overreacted." She climbed in. Cash rested his forearms on the top of the open door. She explained, "I go on intuition a lot in dealing with kids, and his certainty really shook me. I guess he needs to believe in something. Nobody believes in him."

"What's he like?" Cash asked.

"Why?"

"Just curious."

"Oh well, he's very tall and lanky. He has a sensitive face and hair very... very much like yours."

"Athletic?"

"No, I guess his health problems kept him from Little League and all that. But he's musical. He played rhythm guitar with a group called The Sophisticates before he moved here. He's very bright and wants to go to college. He could have, too."

"Could have?"

"I'm not sure he has the discipline now or that he can make up for his lack of basic knowledge. He's spent too many years being knocked around and feeling he isn't worth anything. I'm sure the families he lived with did their best to make him feel loved, by and large. But he started out knowing he didn't belong to anyone. It's a hard thing to overcome. He wouldn't have accepted affection easily."

"Is there anything at all about his real parents in his record?"

"No, he was left at an orphanage when he was a newborn. He's a foundling."

"Where?"

"Chicago," Meg said.

"Chicago... then there aren't any siblings?"

"None that I know of."

Cash nodded slowly and shut the car door. Meg rolled down the window. "I'd better go over some notes for my speech," he said. "See you Thursday?"

"Okay." She kissed a finger, touched it to his cheek.

He started to turn away, then paused. "Do you happen to remember his birthday?"

"Why in the world would you want to know that?"

"We've been talking about the circumstances of his birth, haven't we?"

"October. He'll be seventeen. I don't remember the day," she answered.

"Okay. Just wondered."

He stayed in the parking lot and watched her drive away, the mercury vapor lights overhead shadowing his face strangely. As she pulled into the street, he solemnly raised an arm in farewell. It was the first time she had ever seen him look lonely.

CHAPTER TEN

WHILE SHE WAITED for Cash to answer his phone, Meg propped the receiver on her shoulder and hoisted herself up to sit on the kitchen counter. That reminded her of the morning so long ago when Cash had sat her there and made breakfast, after they'd met jogging. Little had she known that months later they would still be together and in love. It was a dream come true. Still, at odd moments, more dream than reality...

Someone picked up Cash's receiver.

"Delaney residence," a voice clipped. "Brenda Garrison speaking."

Brenda again. It had been Brenda who had answered in Hadley, in Kickapoo, in Morrison. For a split second, Meg regretted that it was not her role to smooth Cash's path. It could have been if she had been willing to drop every thing for him, willing to subordinate her life to his...

"Hi, it's Meg. Sorry to be a pest, but may I speak to Cash?"

"I'm afraid not. He's in the shower."

He was so inaccessible these days! Was it the campaign entirely? Or was he letting her know that he preferred a woman who was at his beck and call?

"Brenda, did you give him my message?"

"Yes I did. He'll get back to you when he can."

It was like talking to a computer. "I've been at meeting the last two evenings," Meg explained. "I must have missed his calls."

"I don't know whether he phoned you or not," Brenda said. "He's very busy. It's only two weeks till the election, you realize."

"Maybe I could run over. I live only a few blocks away."

"I wouldn't advise that. He has a meeting here in half an hour."

Meg put all of her irritation into a sigh.

Brenda's composure broke. "Look, Meg, there's nothing personal in this. It's just wild around here. Somebody has to run interference for him. About an hour ago I had to chase off some kid who was banging at the door, demanding to speak to Cash. He wouldn't deal with anybody else. It was crazy. I had to threaten to call the police. For all I know, he's still out there, waiting for us to leave the house."

"Big tall boy? Black hair?"

"Yes! Do you know him?"

"I'm afraid so," Meg replied. "Did you mention it to Cash?"

"Certainly not. I'm trying to insulate him from that kind of thing."

"Mention it. Please, Brenda. Tell him it was Paul Ward."

"Is it important?"

"Cash doesn't think so. I do. Tell him—tell him I

have a funny feeling about this, like I had about Jessie in Washington. Promise?"

Pause. "I promise." Another pause. Meg felt a truce hanging in the air. "You know about the rally?" Brenda offered in a nicer tone.

"Yes. Thanks. And take care of yourself, Brenda." They would never be friends, Meg thought as she hung up, but both of them cared too much about Cash's welfare to start a war.

At seven that evening, she pressed the last seam of the ice-blue dress she had made to wear to the rally and to the party afterward. She put it on and went across the hall.

"Beautiful!" Ruth exclaimed. "Need any jewelry?"

"I'm just going to wear my aquamarine ring. My birthstone." She twirled around again. "This will be the first time I've appeared in public with Cash. I'm joining him after his speech. I want to keep it simple."

"You'll do all right. How are things going at school? I never see you anymore."

"Fine. Look, I'll talk to you later. I've got to run."

But everything was not fine. As she drove downtown, Meg went over the case of Paul Ward again. He was in less trouble these days, but only because he had withdrawn into himself. She had seen him in her office twice more. He had been civil enough, but also too clever to reveal anything he didn't want her to know. He had refused to talk about Cash. But that Saturday afternoon, when she'd run into him in the public library...

He had been coming out of the newspaper archives with a folder under his arm. Later she recalled seeing newspaper clippings sticking out of it. Still later, when she was looking for a particular back issue of the *Gazette*, she had discovered holes cut in many pages. It hadn't taken much research to learn that the missing articles concerned Cash. Now, she turned down Main Street. She hadn't told Cash about the newspapers. They would only reinforce his crackpot theory, and maybe he was right. Paul Ward was a time bomb looking for a place to explode. Could she defuse him? Could anything but the truth about his parentage defuse him?

At the door of the rally, a young man from Cash's district office stepped up to her. "Meg Birdsong? We have a seat reserved for you up front."

A local candidate for sheriff was talking statistics onstage as she took a seat next to Joe Ignasiak. From the stage, Cash winked at her. He sat with a number of local candidates and dignitaries. The large hall was full. She had read that some candidates had been leery of appearing with Cash after his break with DeWitt. Public attendance, however, had increased everywhere he went.

The candidate for sheriff sat down to generous applause. In the orchestra pit, a well-known businessman struck up a ragtime version of "Happy Days Are Here Again" on the piano. Another speaker took the podium. Meg looked over the noisy crowd. Everybody was having fun; they all smelled victory. When Cash was introduced, the only crowd noise she had ever heard to match the din was in her senior year of high school, at the state high school basketball championship.

Smiling, Cash raised his hands for silence, then gripped the edges of the podium and leaned forward slightly to begin. He looked different from everybody else on the stage. He was unique. Charisma, Meg thought: the ability to project one's uniqueness in such a way that others can share it and feel unique themselves. She understood it at last.

He was looking at her as he began his speech. Charisma or no, the message in his eyes was strictly personal.

From the back of the hall, a voice rang out. Meg thought she understood, "I have a question for you!" She knew the voice. Turning, she half rose out of her seat.

Paul Ward waved his long arms, crossing and uncrossing them over his head like a man trying to stop a train that was running him down. He stood backed up against the center pair of double doors, shouting in a ragged voice, fast and garbled. Meg caught, "... seventeen years ago ... want to know the truth..."

A woman behind Meg said in a rich, satisfied voice like plum pudding, "They're all on drugs these days. I think they should close down the schools and put them to work."

Meg tried to get Cash's attention. But his eyes were on two security guards. He blinked once. The guards rushed Paul. As they got hold of his arms, the double doors gave backward and all three stumbled out into the lobby. The doors swung shut on muffled curses.

Joe was on his feet. Meg pulled him back down. "I'll take care of it," she whispered, and slipped down the aisle. Cash was calming the crowd with a quip, drawing them back to him.

The lobby was empty. She hurried outside. The guards were wrestling Paul down the steps. He swung clumsily at one of them, threw himself off balance, and fell heavily against a metal handrail. They leaped at him.

"Leave him alone," Meg ordered sharply. "I'll take responsibility for him." The struggle halted, but nobody let go. "I'll answer to Mr. Delaney. *Let the boy go.*"

They did. The larger of the two men pointed a finger at Paul. "Don't try it again."

Paul sat down fast, holding his side. Meg joined him on the steps, which were ice cold. He looked as if he was going to be sick. His face was shiny with sweat and deathly pale. His eyes were huge and scared, like a hunted animal's. He breathed hoarsely and stared out into the street.

The guards trudged back inside.

A siren wailed in the directon of the interstate. In the locksmith's shop across the street, a man sat under a single light bulb, repairing something. Paul's breathing evened out. Meg wished she had her coat.

"What're you doing here?" Paul asked.

"I'm a friend of Mr. Delaney's. Yes, really. That's why Mr. Stanley sent you to me instead of to Mrs. Mueller, the other counselor."

"Whyn't you tell me?"

"It never came up," Meg said. "I wasn't hiding it."

"You talk to him about me?"

"Yes, I have."

"Is he my father?"

"He says he isn't, Paul. I believe him."

He made a cynical noise and cracked his knuckles. She thought he was going to cry, but he didn't. She wanted to cry for him.

"Can I give you a lift home?" she asked.

"I guess." He was shivering too, all his fight gone.

"Your folks are home, aren't they?"

"No."

"Where are they?"

"Euchre tournament. They'll be home late." He hung his head. "I don't want them to know about this. Jeez."

Meg rummaged in her purse and came up with a drycleaning receipt and a lipliner. On the back of the receipt she wrote, *That was Paul Ward. He shouldn't be alone. I'll stay with him till he's okay. Call my apt. Meg.*

"I have to go back inside a second, Paul. Promise me you'll wait for me here? We need to talk."

He didn't move. She looked back at him once. When he filled out, he'd be a big man—almost as big as Cash. Right now he just looked young and lost.

Inside, Cash was still speaking. The young man from the district office was still hanging around the door.

"Can you deliver this message to Mr. Delaney?" she asked him. "It's urgent."

"Now?"

"Yes."

"No way." He took the note and stuffed it in his breast pocket. "Later."

"No!" Meg hissed. "Right now. Immediately. It's not that I don't trust you, but I can't take any chances."

"Sorry."

She had another of her intuitions and knew she wasn't lying when she said, "It could mean the election."

The young man tapped his foot, and his face went blank. Ignore it and it'll go away, his expression said.

"Go on," she goaded him. "It'll add a touch of drama. The audience will be impressed with the arrival of a message. It'll sharpen their attention."

"Delaney'll have my butt in a sling."

"No, he won't. He needs to know this. Anyway, blame it on me. I'll take the heat. Wait a minute." She rushed to the lobby and looked outside. Paul was still sitting on the steps, staring straight ahead. She rushed back. "Please." Her teeth chattered from nerves and cold. The young man sighed hugely and took the note. Stiffly, he made his way along the wall of the auditorium and through a door that led backstage. Meg had just decided that he'd left by a back exit when he came out of the wings and went to Cash. With a nod, Cash took the note, slipped it in his pocket, and went on speaking.

"Oh no!" she groaned. Remembering Paul, she didn't wait to thank her messenger.

Paul was standing, stamping his feet. His hands were crammed into his pants pockets, and one bony shoulder was shoved higher than the other. She had won the first battle: He had waited for her.

In the car, she said, "I've been trying to think what's the right thing to do. What do you want from Mr. Delaney?"

"I dunno. To talk to him." He sat hunched over, like some wild, unkempt bird.

"To talk about being his son?"

"I don't care if I'm his son or not." He turned his face to the window and muttered an obscenity.

"I see. I guess I thought you did care."

"I just want to know the truth, that's all."

"How different do you think your life would be if he were your father?" Meg asked.

"I don't want anything from him! I know what you think. You think I want money, a free ride. That I'm some kind of creep that bothers people!"

"All right. You'll get to talk to him. I guarantee it." They listened to the radio for the rest of the ride.

A shadow of apprehension crossed her mind when they got to her apartment. She didn't really know the boy. She had just seen him be disorderly in public. He outweighed her, as thin as he was, by forty pounds. Yet all her instincts insisted that he was not disturbed, but lonely; not irrational, but trapped in an irrational situation. All the same, she didn't bolt the door. The kind of juvenile delinquent that so many people secured their homes against, was inside with her.

"Have a seat. I'll make some cocoa," she said. After she set the milk to heating, she phoned the hall where the rally was. No answer. She phoned Paul's home. No answer. She couldn't remember the name of the people who were giving the party after the rally. She thought of phoning Jonathan, but decided to wait.

When she brought in the cocoa, Paul was sitting in the willow chair with her unabridged dictionary open on his knees. "Looking for a particular word?" she asked.

"No." His eyes danced over the page. "I used to read the dictionary all the time."

"Do you have one?" She took a seat.

"I used to. There was a fire in one place I lived."

She nodded, understanding. He led one of those marginal lives in which tragic mistakes occurred more frequently than the norm. These were the lives that filled the police blotter with deaths due to faulty space heaters, cheap wiring, bald tires, unsafe working conditions. They were the mistakes of poverty and fatigue, not of bad judgment. She wished she could show him the way out. He deserved better. She reached for the sweater lying on the coffee table and shrugged it on. They all deserved better. They were all worth saving, one at a time.

"Paul, besides the letter, is there anything else that makes you think Mr.—that Cash is your father?"

He drank greedily, like a child, wiped the back of his hand across his mouth, and then wiped his hand on his knee. "There was this sister in the Catholic school I went to once."

"What about her?"

"She was real old and sort of nutty. The kids made fun of her, but I sort of liked her." The spots of red on his cheeks were alarming. "She worked in the library." He went back to perusing the dictionary.

"She worked in the library."

"Yeah well, she was always recommending books for me to read. She's the reason I like to read. And one time I was expelled for a week for getting into a fight. So when I got back to school, Sister Margaret says to me that I need to stay in line and try to make something of myself because my father's an important man and someday maybe I'll get to meet him and he should be proud of me." He squirmed in his chair.

"Did she say who your father was?"

"Nah. She was nutty. But there was something about the way she told me. I couldn't forget, you know? So when the letter came, it seemed like Sister Margaret was right."

"How old were you when she told you this?"

"I don't know. Eleven, maybe. It was just like those legends she gave me to read, you know? Some peasant finds out he's a prince. That's probably where she got the idea." He closed the dictionary. "Can we talk about something else?"

Cash would have been starting his first term then, Meg thought. "I'm still trying to get in touch with Cash. I was hoping he'd call."

Paul stood up. "He's not going to talk to me. This is a waste of time."

"Both of you need to hear what the other has to say. I wonder if you've thought about how damaging your story might be to his campaign—if the wrong people got hold of it."

"I'm leaving."

"Let me try one more time." She kept an eye on him as she dialed. He was calm now. She could trust him not to do anything crazy. As he roamed the living room, flipping through magazines, reading the backs of record jackets, whistling through his teeth, he looked like any other restless teenager. When she returned, he was leaning on the ironing board she hadn't had time to put away. "No luck."

All at once he grinned like a little kid and lifted her steam iron over his head. "Hey, pumping iron."

"Not bad." She laughed.

"You're not steamed?"

"No, but I'm pressed for time." They both groaned. "Come on, Paul, I'll take you home. But tomorrow—"

The door burst open. Paul froze with the iron held high. Cash was a blur across the room. He tackled Paul, and the two of them crashed to the floor, knocking a leg off the coffee table. The iron sailed into the glass front of the bookcase and shattered it. After that, it was very still. Then Paul started to cough. Cash sat up, holding a fistful of Paul's jacket with one hand and rubbing his shoulder with the other.

"I don't believe you two have met," Meg observed.

"Call the police," Cash ordered, panting.

"I'd prefer to introduce you myself. Cash, Paul. And vice versa."

"He was about to brain you with that iron!"

"He was not."

Cash got to his feet. "You're not a hostage?"

"Certainly not."

"Oh." He brushed glass off his suit and took Paul's elbow to help him up.

"If anybody's a hostage, it's Paul," Meg explained. "I brought him here to wait while I tried to get in touch with you or his family. Didn't Brenda tell you about this afternoon?"

"No."

"Damn."

Cash said, "I didn't look at your note till I got to the Ericksons'. When I didn't see you after the rally, I thought you'd join me there. The note made me think you were in trouble." He stuck out a hand to Paul. "Sorry."

"Yeah." Like everybody who met Cash for the first time, Paul was mesmerized. But he had more reason to be.

They all sat down, Cash in the willow chair, Paul on one end of the couch, and she on the other. That was when she noticed that Cash was mesmerized, too. He couldn't take his eyes off Paul. "Meg has told me about you." He was uncharacteristically hesitant. "Do you still have that letter about your... background?"

"Yeah."

"Where?"

"At home."

"I'd like to see it. Tonight," Cash said.

Paul shrugged. His mouth was tight and his expression surly.

"Why not?" Cash asked.

"I'm not your son."

Cash sat back in his chair. "Then what is all this about?"

"I thought I was." Paul was sweating again. Meg wanted to run out of the room and leave him in peace. "That's why I tried to bust up that meeting tonight. But

I figured out something, see. Just now."

"What's that?" Cash asked.

"It's what she said." Paul glanced at Meg. "This would be bad publicity for you. It's a setup. They're trying to get at you. I'm just a tool."

"Who's they?"

"I don't know," Paul replied. "But it makes sense."

"It does, in a way," Cash mused.

Abruptly, Paul flung himself off the couch and lunged for the door.

"Wait a minute." Cash went after him. "If this is a setup, then they aren't through with you."

"Big deal."

"Bigger than you may think."

"So?"

"We'll talk about it. I'll drive you home."

"Suit yourself." Paul slouched out.

Cash followed him, then stuck his head around the door. "I'll be back." The look of intensity and determination on his face was awesome. "Lock the door."

After she swept up the glass, Meg put some Chopin on the stereo and curled up on the couch with her shoes off. She thought about Paul riding in the Continental, imagined the picture the two of them would make—the arrogant-looking handsome man in his pin-striped suit and the gangly, poorly dressed youth who had a spark of the same arrogance in his clouded eyes. She listened to four sides of Chopin before Cash rapped at the door.

"Phone call," he said, kissing her on the cheek before continuing into the kitchen. She heard him talking to Brenda. When he returned, he sat down beside her and put a hand on her knee. "Pretty dress. I'm sorry you didn't get to show it off. We'll go out to dinner soon."

"Don't worry about that. What did you think of Paul?"

"Bright. Confused. A smartass." Cash stared through the far wall.

"Can I get you anything?" She loosened his tie and unbuttoned his collar button.

He didn't hear her. "Let me tell you a story. An old story." He stroked her knee absently, as if he were alone with a sleeping pet. The story came out slowly, with many pauses. "When I was a senior in college, I met a girl from Illinois in my English history class. It was a novelty, meeting somebody from Illinois in the East, and I guess she reminded me some of my farm relatives. Her name was Cheryl. She was wholesome, very sweet-tempered, and shy. Different from the drop-dead sophisticates I'd been involved with up till then. We started dating. Our backgrounds were very different. She was solid lace-curtain Irish from Chicago, a strict Catholic. On scholarship. I had money, appetites to spend it on, a fast crowd of friends, some of whom I'd known in prep school. She was a very sweet girl. Quite a woman now, I guess." He was no longer with Meg. He was back in the golden shadows of that other time.

"And one day," Meg said softly.

"Yes, one day she found out she was pregnant. There was snow on the ground, I remember. I was writing my senior thesis. We took a long walk along the river. We felt like we'd never met before."

"What were your options?"

"There weren't any. She went home for spring break and never came back. Today it would be different. But then, the sexual revolution was pretty much a guerilla war. By the time you got to college, people were more open."

He pushed the broken coffee table away with his foot and stretched out his legs. "I offered to marry her, but neither set of parents would consider it. Mine didn't want me tied down at that stage of my life. Hers were angry and embarrassed, didn't want anything to do with me. Cheryl didn't know what she wanted. I think she really wanted marriage, but she was afraid I was only doing my duty by asking her. We never got to finish discussing it, but I'll admit that later I was relieved it never came to pass. I was twenty-one. All of my friends were going to graduate school, Europe, New York, or Vietnam after graduation. Almost nobody was getting married. Whether marriage would have worked for us or not, I don't know. We loved each other. But both of us still had a lot of growing up to do, and in different directions."

"Did you ever see her again?"

"I intended to go up to Chicago during spring break to see her, but she phoned to tell me she was going on a trip. When I got back to school, she had withdrawn from all her classes. Nobody knew anything. Her parents told me she had gone to relatives in Denver to have the baby. The next time I was in Chicago, I looked them up to get her address. They told me she had had a miscarriage and that she was going to school on the West Coast. She was starting a new life and they said she wanted to be left alone. By that time, I agreed with them. It had been a college love affair, and college was over. I suppose that sounds cold to you, Meg. What can I say? I believed her parents when they assured me she was through with me. But now..."

"Now you're thinking that she did have the baby."

"Possibly. Paul's the right age. But whether he's our son or not is still very much an open question. There's something funny about it. Why does he turn up now? I'd like to see his file."

It's confidential. You'd have to get a release signed." She weighed the matter of confidentiality. "I've seen the file of course. There's not much there."

"Then I'll have to find Cheryl." He scratched his jaw. "I haven't thought of her in years."

Our son. Cheryl. Our son. The neon words blinked in Meg's mind. She imagined a wheat-colored girl running barefoot through a field of flowers under the wide prairie sky. "How will you find time? You're busy every second until the election."

"I'll have to find time." The lines in his face seemed to deepen.

"What do you mean?"

He put his arm around her. "Will you stand by me no matter what happens?"

"You know I will."

"I wonder if you realize what I'm asking. I even wonder if I do."

She clutched his shirt front. "I'm afraid. Your face frightens me."

"No, no." He kissed her eyelids. "Don't be afraid. We'll get through this."

She laid her head on his shoulder. "I can't help it. I don't know why. I'm not afraid for myself, only for you." He stirred. "Please don't go. "

"No tonight we belong together," he said in a husky voice.

Their lovemaking had never been so thorough and tender, a slow unfolding of such sad, rich beauty that she could not imagine any human pleasure beyond it. Yet they were not alone. Shadows watched them: the wheat-colored girl; Jonathan; Marcia; even David, Meg's ex-husband; and a score of other spectral memories. As they lay tangled blissfully together, falling asleep, Meg understood that an era of innocence in their relationship had drawn to a close. Whatever lay ahead would be different. She could only hope that they themselves would not change. She dreamed about the wheat-colored girl, who sometimes was a stranger and sometimes was herself.

When she awoke the next morning, Cash was gone. The room was stone cold in the bitter early light. The note on his pillow said, *I love you.*

CHAPTER ELEVEN

"COME IN, BABE." Cash pulled her inside, kissed her quickly, and steered her into the living room, where October's bright blue weather filled the bay window.

"What is it? You sounded strange on the phone." She peered into the dining room. "Don't tell me you're alone, for once."

"I wanted to see you first, before the others." But he hardly seemed to be aware she was there. Head tilted in thought, hands in pockets, he paced to the bookcases, then frowned at them as if he had expected something else to be in that location.

Meg took a chair. "What is it?"

He turned abruptly and fixed her with a stare that didn't see her.

"It wasn't that hard to find out about Paul, especially since somebody had already been asking questions. It's not the story I expected to find, however." He waved a hand. "Cheryl didn't get along with her parents, so she went to Chicago to stay with her sister until the baby was due. Denver was a lie. I talked to Janet, the sister, yesterday. She was only twenty-three at the time and barely able to support the two of them. The baby was born at home, with a midwife in attendance, and then Janet took it directly to a Catholic orphanage. She simply left it there, anonymously."

"Paul."

"Yes, it was Paul. He's my son."

Meg avoided his eyes. There was too much emotion in his voice. "Why didn't Cheryl ask you for help?"

"I don't know. But Janet remembers that she was adamant about not contacting me."

"Girls often feel it's all their fault, especially if their families aren't supportive," Meg offered. "I see a lot of that."

"But *I* would have been supportive. I'm sorry she didn't know that," he said. He sat down in the chair opposite Meg's. "Cheryl did go to California. That part was true. She married. No children. About five years ago, she was killed in a skiing accident."

Meg slid out of her chair and knelt at Cash's knees. Somehow it didn't bring her any nearer to him. He was like a statue in a glass case. She could see him, touch him, but he couldn't hear or feel anything from her. "I'm so sorry. How do you feel?"

He put a hand gently on her head. "It's hard to say. I knew her so long ago. Janet says that Cheryl's marriage was very happy."

"Did she ever try to see Paul?"

"For a while she kept in touch with a Sister Margaret who knew him, though she wasn't supposed to." His jaw tightened. "Her parents are still living, but they forfeited their chance to him long ago. They'd better not get in my way now."

"What are you going to do?"

"Acknowledge him."

"Of course. But surely not now. It's only eight days until the election."

Cash took her face in his hands and searched it with troubled eyes; but he was still on the other side of an invisible wall. "It's seventeen years too late for Paul."

"Yes, but—"

"I know all the arguments, Meg. In a few minutes, my staff will be here to make them all over again. But I'm doing the right thing; and in a way, I have you to thank."

"Me?"

He nodded. "I'm not the same man I was in the spring, the man who hid a divorce to win a primary. Knowing you has had a lot to do with the change."

"I didn't make you honest. You've always been that."

"Honest, but not courageous enough. I was letting ambition lead me astray too often, thinking to myself that someday I'd make amends. Now that day has come. You've helped me put the moral choice before the political choice again." He kissed her forehead solemnly. "Thank you, whatever happens."

She rested her cheek on his knee and tried to put it all in perspective. She couldn't. "Have you talked to Paul? Is this what he wants?"

"He and his family were here earlier. The publicity's going to be tough on him for a while. We talked about sending him to prep school out of the state after I have custody. It'll prepare him for college and give him a new start. We'll see. He has an unusually good relationship with this family, despite his problems in school. That's why he was allowed to move around the state with them. I don't want to take him away from that too fast." He stroked her hair, and his voice was filled with wonder. "But I have a son, Meg. I have a son..."

She bowed her head. For some reason she didn't want to examine, she couldn't bear to look at his face.

The doorbell chimed. When they had all arrived, there

were six of them. Meg knew only Brenda and Roger. Nobody liked Cash's news.

A beefy man named George exploded. "It's got to be buried and buried deep. Does the sister want money? Can we send the kid somewhere until after the election?"

"The sister didn't find me. I found her," Cash snapped. "Nobody's going to be paid off."

"But this is insane. You can't trot out an illegitimate son a week before the election and expect people to swallow it. That's not the way these things work!" George spit into the empty fireplace.

"He's right," Brenda fretted. "Can't you just hold off until after the election?"

"You people are missing an important point," Cash said. He and Meg sat on the couch now, holding hands. "I've insisted all along that Paul's appearance in Masefield at this particular time was too neat. And we've wondered, all of us, what Sam DeWitt was going to do about my break with him. Haven't we been waiting for the other shoe to fall? DeWitt can't use Saunders. Saunders is a woolly-brained liberal. He's everything Sam dislikes."

Meg dug Cash in the ribs for that slur on his opponent, whom she respected.

"DeWitt brought Paul to Masefield?" Roger asked.

"I don't have hard evidence yet. I may never have it. Sam's too smart to leave tracks. But Paul's foster father, William Denton, told me that the job offer here came out of the blue. A man appeared at his house one day with the details, having traveled across the state. Denton didn't stop to ask questions. The money was too good."

"Okay," Roger argued. "So Sam finds your son and gets him moved into your political district. Then what?"

"Then," Cash resumed, "it gets very simple. Just before the election, he breaks the story that the wealthy congressman who pretends to care about the unfortunate has an illegitimate son living in relative poverty not ten blocks from him. What they'll say about Paul's mother I'd hate to guess." He looked at each person in turn. "Are you beginning to understand? I'd like to think that I'd do the right thing by Paul in any case. But the fact is, a decent person has little choice. I figure that we're only hours ahead of Sam's bombshell. If I want to preserve any dignity at all, I have to announce it before he does. The only other option is to deny the story. To lie."

Someone asked, "Can't you just deny it until—"

"No!" Cash roared. He looked down at Meg. "That's what Sam thinks I'll do; try to ride this out and shove Paul back where he came from. If I were that kind of man, then Sam's kind of man could beat me. But not now. Not anymore."

"Let's not be hasty," George grumbled. "We can sleep on it."

"No we can't. There isn't time. I've called a press conference. They should be arriving any time."

After that it was chaotic. Brenda ran to the telephone. The doorbell started ringing. Cash huddled with Roger and another man. The press arrived and set up on the front steps. Passersby collected around the steps and across the street. Doors banged. New people wandered in and out. Cash disappeared. Meg retreated to a corner.

"Ready to roll!" a voice outside shouted. "Where is he?"

Meg started for the front door.

"Hold it." George and Brenda blocked her way.

"The press conference is about to start," Meg protested.

"Go home and watch it on television," George retorted.

Brenda trembled with rage. "None of this would have happened if it hadn't been for you. If he loses, it's going to be on your head."

"That isn't true!"

"You pushed that boy on him," Brenda insisted. "Don't

you see how obvious it is? You're Paul's counselor. And this isn't the first trouble you've caused."

"I wouldn't be surprised if you weren't hooked up with DeWitt," George declared.

"That's crazy!" Heads turned. Meg lowered her voice. "I had nothing to do with Cash's decision." But she did, in a way they wouldn't even try to understand.

"Little lady,"—George gripped her shoulder with a hamlike hand—"Cash was a politician's politician until he got messed up with you. Now he don't know where straight up is. You get the hell out of here. And stay out."

"I'm proud of him," Meg said shakily, "and you should be too. Remember Henry Clay? 'I would rather be right than be president'? That's the kind of spirit Cash is showing."

"What I remember about Henry Clay," George drawled, "is that he never got to be president."

Meg looked to Brenda for help. But the younger woman looked back at her with eyes of ice. "Either way, Meg, it's over for you. If he loses, he'll see what a fool he's been because of you. If he wins, some very influential people are going to make their continued support of him contingent on getting rid of you. I'll see that they do. Why don't you go now, on your own, and save everybody a lot of trouble?"

Meg turned and left the living room. Out of the corner of her eye, she saw Cash in the foyer, ready to go outside and face the reporters. He didn't see her. He was beyond them all now, alone with his destiny. She walked dazedly down the narrow hallway leading to the kitchen and to the back door. It was the worst moment of her life, she thought with eerie detachment. Worse than the night David had told her he was leaving her. Brenda and George were right. She had influenced Cash to be unrealistic. Now he was going to step outside and destroy his career.

Just before she got to the back door, she came to

another door, on the left. It stood ajar. Inside was a room she'd never seen before. It seemed to beckon to her, to promise escape. A fire burned in a wide brick fireplace. A fur throw, bearskin she thought, lay on the polished hardwood floor in front of it. Low, comfortable chairs were scattered about. A decanter of what had to be Scotch sat on a liquor cabinet surrounded by heavy crystal glasses. A book of Walker Evans photographs lay on a table. It was different from the other rooms, more private and somehow more sensual, although she wasn't sure what made it so. Perhaps it was the fire and the many textures. It was a room to run your hands over. She stepped inside and closed the door behind her. Then she saw the television. She felt hollow. It was no use trying to run away. She switched it on, and Cash's face leaped out at her.

"—occasion of great personal satisfaction for me, yet one that requires a careful explanation to the people of my district," he was saying.

She sank to her knees on the bearskin, hypnotized by the strength radiating out of him like the dawn. Yet at the same time, he looked like a man who knew he was trading all his tomorrows for this brief, shining moment.

His prepared statement was over quickly. Then they went at him. Every question tore through her heart like a bullet. Yet she couldn't stop watching. Hardly aware of what she was doing, she threw another log on the fire and sat down again, arms hugging her legs, chin on knees. The scene shifted from the front steps to a panel of hastily assembled analysts in a television studio. She dimly heard noises somewhere in the house, then silence. The analysts set to like starving men at a banquet, tearing at the story with bare hands. The local news followed, with Cash's announcement as the lead story. A camera caught Sam DeWitt entering a restaurant, showing his teeth like an alligator.

"No comment," he grated. "Mr. Delaney has said it all."

She jumped when the door opened.

Cash stood there in his chocolate velour robe, comb marks fresh in his wet hair, holding a snifter of brandy. He was barefoot. He looked as startled as she felt. "Brenda said you'd gone."

"I meant to. I lost track of the time." She swallowed, looked around for a clock. There was none. "You've had time to shower."

"Yes. It was over pretty fast." He drifted into the room, swirling the brandy.

"You didn't bring DeWitt into it. You never mentioned him. That was . . . noble."

"It would only have clouded the issue. Paul's my son, not Sam's."

She ached for him. She didn't know what to do. "Is everyone gone?"

"Rats leaving a sinking ship."

"I'm not a rat."

He walked over to her and looked down at her with narrowed eyes, trying to figure her out. "But they said you'd left for good."

"I should have." She watched the fire, wanting to touch him, but afraid to reach out.

"Go ahead," Cash said. "I've seen it happen before. It happens a lot in politics."

"What does?" She stroked the fur, watched the fire.

"When you lose an election, you lose people, too. People who were closer than your family. And you can't blame them. You're not the winner they thought they were buying into."

"You haven't lost yet."

He laughed shortly. "I've done everything I can to lose. If I don't, then there's no justice in this world."

"And you think that if you lose, I'll leave you?"

"I'm telling you that you can if you want."

She flung her arms around his legs. "Now who's being a martyr? I love you. And as far as I'm concerned, you proved yourself a winner today. I won't leave!" The heat of his thigh against her cheek suddenly focused her confused emotions into desire, and she clung tighter.

He knelt, slipping down through the circle of her arms. "Wait and see," he advised gravely. "Wait until after the election. I may seem like a totally different person then." He set down the brandy and almost reluctantly put his arms around her.

"You don't understand! I was going to leave because this is all my fault! That's what everybody says. All the bad publicity in this campaign has been because of me."

"Do you really believe that?"

"Oh, Cash, I don't know what to believe anymore. I'm just so sorry if I've—"

He pulled her closer, until she was kneeling between his knees. "Let me ask it another way. Do you think, as stubborn and unmanageable as I am, that you could convince me to do anything I didn't want to do?"

Their eyes locked. With a jolt, she realized that his isolation was over. He was back. She smiled.

"Well...no."

"Then stop taking the blame for this flap today. I know what I'm doing, Meg. I've never been more certain. You'll see, in the long run."

She caught some of his fearlessness. "All right, then. What can I do to help?"

"Have some brandy."

"I was thinking of a more substantial contribution. Besides, I'm not sure I like brandy."

"But I do," he said, the tightness around his eyes relaxing. "And I want to taste it on your lips. That's all I want right now." He took a sip and handed the snifter to her.

She drank, looking into his eyes. The brandy burned her throat the way the pressure of his knees burned her thighs. She blurted out, "I need you so much. And I can't. I shouldn't."

"Why not?"

"You're fighting for your life. It's selfish of me to cling, to ask anything of you now."

He took the snifter and set it down. Then he kissed her lingeringly. "If your independent soul has finally decided to cling to me, I'm not going to complain. I think I have strength left to handle it." He kissed her again, his lips tender and loving, his hands strong and gentle as he eased her down and sat leaning over her. "I've definitely discovered a new way to enjoy brandy." With a mischievous twinkle, he dipped the tip of his finger in the brandy, outlined her lips with it, and bent over her again. She had never had a man look at her that way before, but she recognized it. It was adoration. The pressure of his lips and the taste of the brandy set up brush fires all over her. She closed her eyes and massaged the nape of his neck with both hands. A brilliant sunset glowed behind her eyelids.

"The only thing is," he whispered, his breath tickling her cheek, "that this makes me want something else."

Eyes still closed, she let go of him and lay back in complete relaxation. "Mmmm?"

"I want to see you lying naked on the fur." Raising her gently, he pulled off her turtleneck and raked his fingers through her tumbled hair, spreading it on her shoulders. She opened her eyes and grinned, feeling deliciously sexy. He grinned back and slipped off her boots and socks. She raised her hips slightly, and he loosened her jeans. They slid off like melted butter. She lay back, head pillowed on arms, one knee up, and watched his eyes roam her. Her bra was nothing but two shallow fans of lace held together by thin straps, her panties two lace triangles on a band of stretch lace.

He kissed her navel. She sighed shakily, moved her hips. "That's one of the sexiest things about you," he raised his head to say. "On the outside you look so shy and retiring. But then there's this secret sensualist underneath." He kissed along the band of her panties.

"Just waiting for you," she whispered, and then moaned as he put a hand on each thigh and squeezed gently, pushing them apart so that he could lie between them. He unhooked the front closure of her bra and tossed the garment away. In the firelight her breasts blushed as if no man had ever touched them before.

"Your skin against the fur, it's—" His mouth went to her breasts, nibbling, enjoying their fullness and sensitivity. With a cry, she half sat up, pulling him to her. Her nipples gleamed wetly. Cash pushed her back down and peeled off her panties. Then, under his touch, her body began to writhe in a voluptuous dance, the fur caressing her backside, multiplying the effect of his hands. She murmured things she had never said out loud, over and over; and his hands answered.

He stripped off his robe and took her in his arms. When they rolled together, pressing feverishly against each other, she entered total sensuality: hot and cool of fire and room, silken fur, his hard body, the taste of brandy and of him, her own body soft and yielding, his lips exploring her, finding everything he wanted to find...

He slid away from her, and she heard a cabinet open. She rolled on her stomach and rested her head on her folded arms. The fur, warmed and slightly moistened by their bodies, rubbing against her front, was another new erotic sensation. He returned with a bottle of lotion. By the label, it was French, jasmine-based, and scandalously expensive. He poured some in his hand and warmed it between his palms.

"I know what you're thinking," he said. He began to rub it on her shoulders, back, and down over her buttocks. God, what hands, she thought in a haze of arousal. They should be insured by Lloyd's of London. "I don't always happen to have this lying around for whoever, Meg. I bought it for you, for a time like this."

"Oh *really?*"

"I hope to hell you don't wear that lacy stuff for anyone else. Do you?"

"Let me think.... No." She chuckled.

"Okay, it's the same thing."

He turned her on her back and spread more lotion over her.

"I can't...argue...right now," she panted shallowly, and wondered if she would ever be able to stop smiling. As he bent nearer, she ran her hands over him, over the awesome physique so finely tuned for physical pleasure.

He lay down again, and they came together passionately. He buried his face against her, inhaling. "Mmmm, yes. I knew this was the perfume for you."

"What makes you such an expert on women's perfume?" She wrapped her legs around his.

"I'm not. I learned about this one from a woman who hugged me at a rally." He punctuated his explanation with short, punchy kisses on and around her lips that made her giggle and toss. "I asked her the name." He kissed her throat and shoulders, paying special attention to the tattoo. "I have licentious thoughts about you at the most inopportune times, my dear. If the public only knew what's behind my friendly smile." He eased himself over her, and they united with that completeness that always took her breath away. His face changed, softened. "I love making love to you."

Moving together, they embarked on a journey without time or thought, only feeling: his body one with hers, in the deep, thrusting union that threatened separation then obliterated it, over and over. She felt herself closing around him, keeping him always with her, at the same time that his power and strength overwhelmed her own, possessing her totally. It could never end, the flow of passion coursing between them; and yet when it did, and she arched up with a cry into the full force of him, it was not like an ending at all, but a birth, a beginning.

They lay heavily together, hearts pounding. A hot, musky jasmine odor filled the room. The fire crackled. At the other end of the world, a doorbell rang. They didn't care. Later they lay on their sides, facing each other. Meg fingered the hair on his chest, smoothing the places where it grew in whorls.

Yawning, he pushed at her hair, arranging a curl here and there. "We're so good together."

She snuggled closer.

He left to build up the fire, then lay down again, pulling her close. "Almost too good." He closed his eyes.

"What do you mean?"

Silence.

"Cash?"

"I don't know. Nothing."

The cold began at her toes and crept upward. She thought about the way some flowers are at their most brilliant just before the killing frost, and she thought about the way Chopin's music, and Mozart's, had used up their creators so young. Did Cash sense some hidden timetable that was pushing their feelings to a white-hot heat, precisely because the end was near?

And then she thought she knew how the end would come. Hadn't it been obvious from the beginning? After the election, she would either be the woman who brought Cash Delaney down or she would be the woman in spite of whom, and with great difficulty, Cash had triumphed. Dread filled her. Tonight they were resting in the eye of the whirlwind. Tomorrow they would plunge back into it; and it would be fiercer than before. They could not possibly stay together. She looked at his closed face. Perhaps they had just shared a farewell. No! It was absurd... and yet... it was not absurd at all.

"You're shivering," he said, drawing her closer. "Let me warm you." And he did, except for a hard, frozen teardrop of fear deep in her heart.

CHAPTER TWELVE

MEG FINISHED MARKING her ballot and pushed back the curtain of the voting booth. A flash camera went off in her face, and she recoiled, then collected herself to smile tightly. Cash came out of the next booth and received the same treatment, which he handled with his customary ease.

"Have any trouble making up your mind?" he teased, reaching for Meg's hand. Together, they deposited their ballots in the ballot box, pausing to let the man with the camera snap another shot.

"Should I be in these pictures with you?" Meg whispered.

"Sure, unless you're afraid of ruining your standing with your liberal friends." He steered her toward the door, nodding at the other early voters and accepting good wishes and handshakes.

A young woman wearing too much lip gloss shoved a microphone under his nose. "Congressman, how do you think the announcement about your illegitimate son will affect the voting today?"

"I'm very proud that Paul is my son. I only wish I had known of his existence earlier." He plowed ahead, cordial but wary, pulling Meg along.

"Yes, but you've dropped eleven percentage points in the polls since your press conference. Do you think the trend will hold?"

"No comment."

Someone held the door. Meg and Cash left the building.

"Do you think your differences with the DeWitt family will affect your ability to carry out your duties if you're reelected?"

Cash opened Meg's door. His nostrils were slightly flared, the skin on either side of them white. To the reporter, he said, "I would suggest you examine my record in Congress. That will tell you how I have fulfilled and will continue to fulfill my duties." He slammed Meg's door and went around the car, the newswoman on his heels. He climbed in.

"Can you comment on your father's—"

"No comment." He slammed that door and started the automobile. "Vultures," he mumbled.

They were almost to Ingersoll School before Meg dared to ask, "Your father?"

"The great untold story of the campaign." He had cooled down. "You live in Illinois. You know the background."

"I know that he and Sam DeWitt are old friends. I know he owns radio and television stations. That's where your family's wealth comes from, doesn't it?"

"Yes. My early opponents used to charge that his control of some of the media gave me an unfair advantage in a campaign." He accelerated to change lanes. "They can't say that this time. He's letting me twist in the wind."

"Look," Meg argued. "I know that an illegitimate son is a shock to a family like yours, but surely he's on your side. You're his flesh and blood."

"Even fathers like to back winners, Meg. Or maybe I should say, especially fathers." He pulled up to the curb behind a school bus. "I've only spoken to him once since Sam and I parted company. It wasn't friendly. That's almost a bigger issue than Paul, for my father."

"It's horrible! Why didn't you tell me?"

He stretched an arm along the back of the seat and leaned a shoulder against the door. "You couldn't have done a thing about it. Anyway, think how many years Paul did without the support of *his* father."

Meg pointed toward the playground. "The day I met you there, I thought you were spoiled, uncaring, hiding weakness behind wealth. How could I have been so wrong? You're the strongest man I've ever known. You aren't afraid of anything."

He looked away, appearing troubled by something new. "You're going to be late for school."

"I want to stay with you today. You know that," she said, vaguely alarmed. "But I have to administer those psychological tests. I'll try to finish early and join you."

"We'll see. I have things to do." He kissed her cheek, avoiding her beseeching gaze.

Meg got out of the car. Something was slipping out of control. Something was happening that she didn't understand. "Cash! I'll—I'll never abandon you!"

His lips thinned briefly. He shifted into drive. "Goodbye, Meg."

"Good . . . luck."

She watched until he was out of sight, then hurried to her office, dazedly dodging students, craving time alone to compose herself. Even now, when Cash needed her most, their separate responsibilities pushed them apart. Unfair, unfair!

The intercom crackled on just as she sat down at her

desk. "Ms. Birdsong, Ms. Birdsong. Report to the principal's office, please."

Mr. Stanley was waiting with a man and a woman who looked to be in their early forties. The man was bearded and wore khaki work clothes. The woman was plump under her old plaid wool coat. She had a round, pleasant face and curly, gray-brown hair.

"Meg," said Mr. Stanley, "this is Bill and Lucille Denton, Paul's foster parents."

Meg stumbled through greetings. "Something's wrong?"

"Yes there is." Lucille Denton leaned forward, gripping her purse with both hands. "When I went in to wake Paul this morning, he wasn't there. He's gone."

"He left a note," Mr. Stanley added.

"It's because of Mr. Delaney," Lucille Denton said. "Paul feels like he's cost him the election. He wants to go away and not bother anybody." She sighed. "At least that's how I understand it."

Mr. Stanley handed Meg a sheet of paper torn from a spiral notebook. Paul's handwriting was spidery and delicately turned.

"He doesn't say where he's gone," Meg noted. "Just that he's going to live with friends."

Bill Denton stopped contemplating his knuckles and looked at her with startlingly blue eyes. "It's all been too much for him. Nobody's to blame."

"Does Cash know?" Meg asked.

"Not yet," Lucille replied. "We didn't think, with the election and all—"

"Good," Meg cut in. "We'll tell him after we find Paul, if then. Have you notified the police?"

"That would only cause more publicity, wouldn't it?" Bill Denton pointed out.

Mr. Stanley offered, "The Dentons think Paul either went to Chicago or to Granite City. He'll be hitchhiking, since he doesn't have much money. I doubt his friends will give him away over the phone. So we'll have to find him ourselves. Meg, if you want to help, I'll get somebody from Westside to do the testing for you. Paul can't have gone far."

In half an hour she had collected the VW and was pulling onto the interstate, headed west. Beside her on the seat was a list of the names and addresses of the members of Paul's old band, The Sophisticates. She began at once to scan the shoulders, ditches, and overpasses for a gangly figure with a backpack. The Dentons would be doing the same on the road to Chicago. The day was cold and clear, and the car heater didn't work. She tried to remember a time when she had felt more frustrated, but she couldn't. At nine, she turned on the radio to catch the news. Suddenly, she heard:

"—too early to tell, but a straw vote taken among voters leaving the polls indicates that Delaney is running surprisingly strong within the city limits of Masefield, where it was thought Saunders would roll up an early lead. In the rural areas, however, where the incumbent has been unbeatable in previous contests, voter turnout promises to be the lowest in several years."

As if she were praying, she said silently, And I should be with you, Cash. Do you know, do you understand, how much I want to be there? But I'm doing this for you...

She recalled his strange mood when they had parted. He was preoccupied, understandably, but there had been something else as well. If only she could go back two hours! She had forgotten to say I love you.

She stopped at every truck stop, but there was no sign of Paul. Twice she phoned Ingersoll, but the Dentons had not checked back yet. When she pulled into Granite City long after noon, a blinding headache pounded behind her eyes. According to the informal polls, Saunders was leading narrowly in Masefield.

One of the Sophisticates had left town. The drummer, whom she found in a high school biology class, thought Paul had gone to New Orleans. The lead singer, working in a body shop, promised to get in touch if he heard from Paul. The last address was incorrect. Around four, she bought a bottle of aspirin and stopped in a diner for a sandwich. From there, she phoned Ingersoll again. Mr. Stanley spoke so loudly that she had to hold the phone away from her ear.

"They found Paul, through his old school in Chicago!"

"How is he?"

"I don't know. They won't get back to town for a while; but he's willing to reconsider his options, apparently. Meg, if it's any consolation, he almost went in your direction. When he got to the interstate interchange, he flipped a coin."

"And the election?"

"It's back and forth. Your congressman telephoned here for you. We were vague as to your whereabouts."

"Okay." Meg sighed. Her headache loosened a notch. "I'm coming home."

Just after dark, she pulled off the interstate for gas at an exit without a town. As she filled the tank, the wind nearly cut her in two. She paid the shivering attendant and turned the key in the ignition.

Nothing happened.

Frantically, she rolled down her window. "Can you see what's wrong? I've got to get to Masefield tonight!"

She waited in the grimy, overheated office.

It took the man two eternities to figure it out. "It's the generator. I'll phone over to Coslow for the part." He considered the clock. "I close at ten."

"Do you have a radio?"

"It's broke."

She paced, read road maps, and hoped that Cash was

Into the Whirlwind

too busy to think of her. Because if he did, he might never forgive her for skipping out on him. If the Dentons decided to keep Paul's escape attempt a secret, then she would never be able to explain. Few customers broke the monotony. The service station manager went home for dinner and was briefly replaced by a teenage girl, who spent the time perfecting her gum-cracking skills. The manager returned. Near closing time, he went out to fill up a station wagon.

In a minute he stomped in, blowing on his hands. "There's some folks out here will take you to Masefield if you want to leave your car till tomorrow. There's no motels around here."

It was a retired couple named Brinkley. Mr. Brinkley wasn't the slowest driver she'd ever known, but a good team of snails could have blown him off the road.

Finally, Meg said, "Do you mind if we turn on the radio? I'd like to hear some election results."

"Why, was it election day?" Mrs. Brinkley asked mildly. She moved dials around. After a bit, a Masefield station came through.

"—here at the Hotel Frederick, where we have Congressman Cash Delaney standing by. Congressman, we understand that with a substantial percentage of the votes counted, Ted Saunders appears to be ahead by a narrow margin."

"That's correct, John." Cash's voice was firm, calm, slightly hoarse.

"Have you spoken with Mr. Saunders this evening?"

"No, I haven't conceded yet," Cash answered, but Meg heard defeat in his voice. Tears stung her eyelids. She bowed her head and shielded her eyes with a hand.

The newsman persisted, "Are you satisfied with the way the campaign has been run? There's been a lot of controversy about that."

"I'm satisfied with the way my opponent and I have

handled ourselves. But as you know, John, since the middle of the campaign, I haven't really been running against Ted Saunders."

"You're speaking of your differences with your original backers."

"Yes, and of public opinion concerning my private life," Cash said.

"Speaking of your private life, Congressman, I understand that you have another concern tonight besides the election."

"That's right." Emotion colored Cash's words. "A...friend of mine, Meg Birdsong, was on her way to Masefield by car from the western part of the state this afternoon and is long overdue to join us. My son, Paul, who is here with me, verifies that she was last heard from hours ago, when she telephoned from Granite City. I've alerted the state police—" His throat closed up.

Mrs. Brinkley turned to peer at Meg. "Is that—?"

"Yes," Meg said. "That's me."

"Jeepers." Mr. Brinkley stepped on the accelerator.

It was past midnight before she was pounding up the staircase of the Hotel Frederick to the grand ballroom, shivering with nervous exhaustion, her hair wild. At the wide doorway, she stopped to catch her breath. Clusters of subdued staffers and friends filled the room under the biggest chandelier Meg had ever seen. Paul and the Dentons stood against the far wall, talking to a handsome, white-haired man. And there was Cash, surrounded by people as always. Both he and Paul looked better than she had expected. She was about to wonder where Brenda was when Cash saw her. She dropped her purse and coat. A path opened between them, like the parting of the Red Sea. The polished floor rang like a bell under her heels as she ran to him. He swept her into his arms.

"Car trouble," she gasped.

"Why didn't you let me know?" he demanded roughly.

"I would have had to explain about Paul, and I wasn't sure you should know and—"

"It doesn't matter." Relief replaced anger, and he hugged her tightly. "But dammit, I imagined all kinds of crazy things. I even thought you'd chosen to disappear, that you knew how the election would go."

"What?" She glared up at him. "That's what was bothering you this morning?"

"You've heard?"

"About the election? Yes." She nodded. "I didn't fall in love with the office. I fell in love with the man."

The room broke into applause. With a blush, she realized how loudly she had spoken.

Cash laughed. "Come over here. There's someone I want you to meet."

He guided her toward Paul's group. The distinguished-looking old gentleman watched her with uncommon attention. Meg smiled at Paul, who looked tired but steady. He had even dressed up a bit, in slacks and a pullover.

Lucille Denton looked five years younger than she had that morning. "We'll talk." She smiled at Meg.

Cash said, "Meg, I'd like you to meet my father."

"We've been worried about you," Delaney Senior rumbled, extending a knotty hand.

"It's nice to meet you, *finally*," she returned.

He raised a bushy eyebrow. "Finally?"

Cash squeezed Meg's shoulder affectionately. "I told you, Dad, this lady doesn't pull any punches."

Delaney Senior fixed her with a steely eye. "You're exactly right that I haven't lent active support in this campaign, as I have in others, my dear. I didn't agree with my son's decision to go it alone, especially against old family friends. But now, I regret to admit that I was wrong. His way was right. That's why I'm here." Embarrassed, he took out his cigarettes.

"But he blew the election," Paul objected.

Cash's father inhaled smoke and addressed the group at large. "It's not that simple. Saunders was expected to carry Masefield, but he didn't do it. Cash, you were expected to show your usual strength in the more conservative outlying areas. Instead, Saunders won there. But *not* because people changed their votes. In fact, it's already clear that your supporters stayed home rather than vote against you. The revelation about Paul here confused them this time. But they'll be back. And you've won over many city voters. I'd say your power base is secure for the future. Saunders's margin of victory is small. Not only that, but if you had won, some people would continue to think that you had made some kind of deal with Sam. Now it's evident that nobody owns you and you've been willing to pay a price for that freedom." The old man's eyes shone. "It's a moral victory, son. And I'm proud of you."

"Moral victories don't put you in office," Cash growled, but Meg could see he was touched.

Cash's father pulled Cash and Meg apart from the others and lowered his voice. "We'll talk tomorrow about the next step. I have some information about a Senate seat becoming available."

Cash's head snapped up. "Amundsen's?"

"Not public knowledge yet," his father murmured. "But I've been approached by a group interested in seeing you run. Not DeWitt, you can be sure."

"Even with this loss?" Cash asked wryly.

"Your destiny isn't a law practice in Masefield," his father said. "You know it. Everybody knows it. This isn't the end. It's a change of direction."

Cash nodded to himself. "Yes, that's what I feel. But I'll need time to think things over."

His father flipped his cigarette into a sand-filled urn. "Take all the time you need. Come and see your mother and me. Anyway, it seems to me you have plenty to do for a while, getting acquainted with your son...my grandson... and—" He glanced at Meg.

"No objections, Dad, if I take on a new staff member?"

Delaney Senior permitted himself the ghost of a smile. "You've always had a talent for convincing the best people to come aboard."

"If she'll have me," Cash remarked with a twinkle in his eye. He turned to Meg. "What about it, Meg? I just lost my job and my politics don't match yours, but I love you. Will you marry—"

A staffer bustled between them, trailed by a television interviewer and cameraman. "We've got Saunders on the line, like you wanted. You ready?"

The interviewer stepped in front of the staffer and held up his microphone. The cameraman slipped in next to him. "Congressman, what are your feelings about this loss? Any immediate plans for the future?"

Cash kept looking at Meg.

"Yes." She smiled at him. "The answer is yes."

Paul moved into the group. Cash put one arm around his son and the other around Meg. He faced the camera. "I've lost this election," he said, "but there will be other elections. And besides"—he looked from Paul to Meg, his eyes shining with love—"I've won everything else."

WONDERFUL ROMANCE NEWS:

Do you know about the exciting SECOND CHANCE AT LOVE/TO HAVE AND TO HOLD newsletter? Are you on our *free* mailing list? If reading all about your favorite authors, getting sneak previews of their latest releases, and being filled in on all the latest happenings and events in the romance world sounds good to you, then you'll love our SECOND CHANCE AT LOVE and TO HAVE AND TO HOLD Romance News.

If you'd like to be added to our mailing list, just fill out the coupon below and send it in...and we'll send you your *free* newsletter every three months — hot off the press.

☐ *Yes, I would like to receive your free SECOND CHANCE AT LOVE/TO HAVE AND TO HOLD newsletter.*

Name _____
Address _____
City _____ **State/Zip** _____

Please return this coupon to:

Berkley Publishing
200 Madison Avenue, New York, New York 10016
Att: Irene Majuk

HERE'S WHAT READERS ARE SAYING ABOUT

"I think your books are great. I love to read them, as does my family."
—*P. C., Milford, MA**

"Your books are some of the best romances I've read."
—*M. B., Zeeland, MI**

"SECOND CHANCE AT LOVE is my favorite line of romance novels."
—*L. B., Springfield, VA**

"I think SECOND CHANCE AT LOVE books are terrific. I married my 'Second Chance' over 15 years ago. I truly believe love is lovelier the second time around!"
—*P. P., Houston, TX**

"I enjoy your books tremendously."
—*I. S., Bayonne, NJ**

"I love your books and read them all the time. Keep them coming—they're just great."
—*G. L., Brookfield, CT**

"SECOND CHANCE AT LOVE books are definitely the best.!"
—*D. P., Wabash, IN**

*Name and address available upon request

NEW FROM THE PUBLISHERS OF *SECOND CHANCE AT LOVE!*

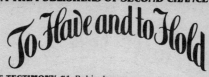
To Have and to Hold™

___	**THE TESTIMONY** #1 Robin James	06928-0
___	**A TASTE OF HEAVEN** #2 Jennifer Rose	06929-9
___	**TREAD SOFTLY** #3 Ann Cristy	06930-2
___	**THEY SAID IT WOULDN'T LAST** #4 Elaine Tucker	06931-0
___	**GILDED SPRING** #5 Jenny Bates	06932-9
___	**LEGAL AND TENDER** #6 Candice Adams	06933-7
___	**THE FAMILY PLAN** #7 Nuria Wood	06934-5
___	**HOLD FAST 'TIL DAWN** #8 Mary Haskell	06935-3
___	**HEART FULL OF RAINBOWS** #9 Melanie Randolph	06936-1
___	**I KNOW MY LOVE** #10 Vivian Connolly	06937-X
___	**KEYS TO THE HEART** #11 Jennifer Rose	06938-8
___	**STRANGE BEDFELLOWS** #12 Elaine Tucker	06939-6
___	**MOMENTS TO SHARE** #13 Katherine Granger	06940-X
___	**SUNBURST** #14 Jeanne Grant	06941-8
___	**WHATEVER IT TAKES** #15 Cally Hughes	06942-6
___	**LADY LAUGHING EYES** #16 Lee Damon	06943-4
___	**ALL THAT GLITTERS** #17 Mary Haskell	06944-2
___	**PLAYING FOR KEEPS** #18 Elissa Curry	06945-0
___	**PASSION'S GLOW** #19 Marilyn Brian	06946-9
___	**BETWEEN THE SHEETS** #20 Tricia Adams	06947-7
___	**MOONLIGHT AND MAGNOLIAS** #21 Vivian Connolly	06948-5
___	**A DELICATE BALANCE** #22 Kate Wellington	06949-3
___	**KISS ME, CAIT** #23 Elissa Curry	07825-5
___	**HOMECOMING** #24 Ann Cristy	07826-3
___	**TREASURE TO SHARE** #25 Cally Hughes	07827-1
___	**THAT CHAMPAGNE FEELING** #26 Claudia Bishop	07828-X
___	**KISSES SWEETER THAN WINE** #27 Jennifer Rose	07829-8
___	**TROUBLE IN PARADISE** #28 Jeanne Grant	07830-1
___	**HONORABLE INTENTIONS** #29 Adrienne Edwards	07831-X
___	**PROMISES TO KEEP** #30 Vivian Connolly	07832-8
___	**CONFIDENTIALLY YOURS** #31 Petra Diamond	07833-6

All Titles are $1.95

Prices may be slightly higher in Canada.

Available at your local bookstore or return this form to:

 SECOND CHANCE AT LOVE
Book Mailing Service
P.O. Box 690, Rockville Centre, NY 11571

Please send me the titles checked above. I enclose _____. Include 75¢ for postage and handling if one book is ordered; 25¢ per book for two or more not to exceed $1.75. California, Illinois, New York and Tennessee residents please add sales tax.

NAME _____

ADDRESS _____

CITY _____ STATE/ZIP _____

(allow six weeks for delivery)   THTH #67

Second Chance at Love®

- ___07246-X **SEASON OF MARRIAGE #158** Diane Crawford
- ___07576-0 **EARTHLY SPLENDOR #161** Sharon Francis
- ___07580-9 **STARRY EYED #165** Maureen Norris
- ___07592-2 **SPARRING PARTNERS #177** Lauren Fox
- ___07593-0 **WINTER WILDFIRE #178** Elissa Curry
- ___07594-9 **AFTER THE RAIN #179** Aimée Duvall
- ___07595-7 **RECKLESS DESIRE #180** Nicola Andrews
- ___07596-5 **THE RUSHING TIDE #181** Laura Eaton
- ___07597-3 **SWEET TRESPASS #182** Diana Mars
- ___07598-1 **TORRID NIGHTS #183** Beth Brookes
- ___07800-X **WINTERGREEN #184** Jeanne Grant
- ___07801-8 **NO EASY SURRENDER #185** Jan Mathews
- ___07802-6 **IRRESISTIBLE YOU #186** Claudia Bishop
- ___07803-4 **SURPRISED BY LOVE #187** Jasmine Craig
- ___07804-2 **FLIGHTS OF FANCY #188** Linda Barlow
- ___07805-0 **STARFIRE #189** Lee Williams
- ___07806-9 **MOONLIGHT RHAPSODY #190** Kay Robbins
- ___07807-7 **SPELLBOUND #191** Kate Nevins
- ___07808-5 **LOVE THY NEIGHBOR #192** Frances Davies
- ___07809-3 **LADY WITH A PAST #193** Elissa Curry
- ___07810-7 **TOUCHED BY LIGHTNING #194** Helen Carter
- ___07811-5 **NIGHT FLAME #195** Sarah Crewe
- ___07812-3 **SOMETIMES A LADY #196** Jocelyn Day
- ___07813-1 **COUNTRY PLEASURES #197** Lauren Fox
- ___07814-X **TOO CLOSE FOR COMFORT #198** Liz Grady
- ___07815-8 **KISSES INCOGNITO #199** Christa Merlin
- ___07816-6 **HEAD OVER HEELS #200** Nicola Andrews
- ___07817-4 **BRIEF ENCHANTMENT #201** Susanna Collins
- ___07818-2 **INTO THE WHIRLWIND #202** Laurel Blake
- ___07819-0 **HEAVEN ON EARTH #203** Mary Haskell
- ___07820-4 **BELOVED ADVERSARY #204** Thea Frederick
- ___07821-2 **SEASWEPT #205** Maureen Norris
- ___07822-0 **WANTON WAYS #206** Katherine Granger
- ___07823-9 **A TEMPTING MAGIC #207** Judith Yates

All of the above titles are $1.95
Prices may be slightly higher in Canada.

Available at your local bookstore or return this form to:

 SECOND CHANCE AT LOVE
Book Mailing Service
P.O. Box 690, Rockville Centre, NY 11571

Please send me the titles checked above. I enclose _____. Include 75¢ for postage and handling if one book is ordered; 25¢ per book for two or more not to exceed $1.75. California, Illinois, New York and Tennessee residents please add sales tax.

NAME_____

ADDRESS_____

CITY_____STATE/ZIP_____

(allow six weeks for delivery)   **SK-41b**